Walker's Runners

Robert Rayner

James Lorimer & Company Ltd., Publishers
Toronto, 2002

James Lorimer & Company Ltd. acknowledges the support of the Ontario Arts Council. We acknowledge the support of the Government of Canada through the Book Publishing Industry Development Program (BPIDP) for our publishing activities. We acknowledge the support of the Canada Council for the Arts for our publishing program.

Cover illustration: Greg Ruhl

Cataloguing in Publication Data

Rayner, Robert, 1946–
Walker's runners

(Sports stories; 55)
ISBN 1-55028-763-X (bound) ISBN 1-55028-762-1 (pbk.)

I. Title. II. Series: Sports stories (Toronto, Ont); 55.

PS8585.A974W34 2002 jC813'.6 C2002-900192-7
PZ7.R2317Wa 2002

James Lorimer & Company Ltd., Publishers
35 Britain Street
Toronto, Ontario
M5A 1R7
www.lorimer.com

Distributed in the United States by:
Orca Book Publishers
P.O. Box 468
Custer, WA USA
98240–0468

Printed and bound in Canada.

Contents

Acknowledgements

Thanks to Nancy and Margaret and my grade six students for responding to an early draft of *Walker's Runners*, and to the people at James Lorimer & Co. for their help and advice in developing it.

The book is, of course, for Nancy.

1

In the Gym

Toby hated the gym.

He hated it for its noise — its triumphant shouts and derisive hoots. He hated it for its smell of mouldering sneakers and frantic sweat. He hated it for what it represented: a shallow comradeship and noisy jockism. He hated it for what he was supposed to do in it: to exert himself, and to run.

And he hated it for the humiliation he feared every time he entered it, the humiliation that awaited him in just a few seconds, unless he could fend it off with a few good wisecracks.

His grade six class was standing in six groups at the end of the gym, five students in each group. Ms. Watkins, the phys. ed. teacher, had pointed to six students and told them they were team leaders, and then each team leader had taken turns choosing whom they wanted on their team. That was humiliation number one. Toby knew he was overweight, and he knew he was slow, and he knew he'd be the last to be chosen.

The class had waited in a sprawling group, some eager, knowing they'd be among the first to be picked, some downcast and embarrassed, knowing they'd be among the last, and even then they'd be chosen reluctantly, with comments like, "I guess I'll have to have ...", and, "Since there's no-one left who's any good, I'll have ...", and, "Oh, miss, do I *have* to have ...?"

Toby had been last.

"Oh jeez, miss, do we *have* to have Toby?"

Ms. Watkins, tall and impressively athletic in her purple tracksuit, nodded sympathetically, but said firmly, "He's the last to be chosen, so I'm afraid you have to take him."

"But he's too slow, and he doesn't care."

Toby thought, *You're right on both counts. I am too slow, and I don't care.* He wasn't proud of being slow, but he was proud of not caring.

"You still have to pick him, even if he is slow, and even if he doesn't care."

Thanks for defending me, Ms. Watkins, Toby thought.

The teacher went on, "But perhaps today Toby will surprise us and show us he does care, and he'll try and speed up." She pointed at Toby. "Toby, join your team."

Ms. Watkins was always pointing. Toby supposed she couldn't help it. She had a bony nose that pointed wherever she looked, and her chin and forehead receded rapidly so that her whole face seemed to point. Then she had a large bosom, which pointed as she marched, shoulders back and posture erect, around the gym and through the hallways. And when she wore shorts for track practice in the spring, her bony knees pointed. She was a pointing machine. She taught phys. ed. in the mornings and French in the afternoons, and when she taught French, she stood at the front of the class and pointed even more than she did in phys. ed., demanding that students respond to her questions in French, recite the vocabulary she had given them for homework, and describe in French what was happening in the pictures in their French books.

"Can we trade him?" asked Nathan, the team leader.

"No."

"Can we give him away? One of the other teams can have him."

"We don't want him. You keep him," the neighbouring team leader said.

Toby wanted to interrupt. He wanted to say, *Have you any idea how you make me feel, treating me as if I'm someone's dirty underwear being passed around, as if you'll catch some sort of disease from me if you get stuck with me on your team?* But he knew there was no point in saying anything. The only thing to do was to let the insults take their course and to get back at his tormentors when he could, in the only way he could, by mocking their keenness.

"Toby is on your team. No more arguing. I'm sure Toby will do his best, even if his best is not up to most of our standards. Isn't that right, Toby?"

"Isn't what right, Ms. Watkins?"

"Don't be impertinent, Toby. Isn't what I just asked you right?"

Toby drew a deep breath. He knew in the end he'd be humiliated, but he knew how to go down fighting.

"Do you mean isn't it right that I'll do my best, or isn't it right that my best isn't up to most of our standards? Because if you mean isn't it right that I'll do my best, I can't say until I know what we're supposed to be doing. And if you mean isn't it right that my best isn't up to most of our standards, well I can't say that either because I don't know what most of our standards are. In fact, if you really want me to answer, I'll need to know—"

"Toby, be quiet."

"—What you mean by 'most'?"

"Toby Morton, stop talking." Ms. Watkins took two steps toward Toby, pointing at him as she advanced.

"And what you mean by 'standards'..."

"Stop this nonsense at once." Ms. Watkins took two more steps toward Toby.

"And who you mean by 'our' — do you mean the students, or yourself, and if you mean both, then are your standards the same as the students' standards?"

"Toby Morton, be quiet!"

Ms. Watkins was now about ten centimetres from Toby's face. She was breathing heavily and her face was red. Toby looked into her eyes — she was only a little taller than he — and smiled.

"Just trying to be helpful, Ms. Watkins," he said, helpfully.

A few students giggled nervously. The class jocks, eager to start, glared at him. Ms. Watkins glared, too, then abruptly marched back to the other students.

"Line up in your teams."

The teams lined up. Toby was last in his line. *Here comes humiliation number two*, he thought. But he knew how to handle it.

"When I say 'go,' the first person in each team runs to the end of the gym, touches the wall, runs back, tags the next person, and goes to the end of the line. The tagged person runs to the end of the gym, touches the wall, runs back, tags the next person, and goes to the end of the line. And so on, until the team is lined up again how they started. Is that clear? Any questions?"

Ms. Watkins looked along the lines of students.

Toby raised his hand.

"This had better be a sensible question, Toby. I'm tired of your time-wasting foolishness."

Toby opened his eyes in wide innocence.

"Well … what is your question?" Ms. Watkins asked.

"Why?" said Toby.

"What do you mean 'why'?"

"Why do we have to run to the end of the gym, touch the wall, run back, tag the next person, and go to the end of the line, then the next person run to the end of the gym, touch the wall, run back, tag the next person, and go to the end of the line, then the next person run to the end of the gym ...?"

Ms. Watkins was advancing on Toby again, pointing as she came. "Stop talking this second" — as she said 'second,' she stabbed the air in front of Toby with her finger — "this *second*, or I'll send you to the principal." She was bright red, and breathing hard, and again only centimetres from Toby. "Do you understand?"

Toby said nothing.

"I said, do you understand?"

Toby remained silent.

"*Toby Morton, I said do you understand?!*"

Toby nodded.

"Then why don't you answer me when I ask you a simple question?"

"You said I was to stop talking 'this second'," Toby stabbed the air with his finger — "and if I didn't stop talking you'd send me to the principal, so I couldn't answer, because I had to stop talking."

Ms. Watkins, shaking her head slowly, took three deep breaths, and returned to the front of the lines.

"Get ready. Get set. Go!"

The first six students, the team leaders, who had crouched in a start position as soon as they heard "Get ready," shot forward. They thundered to the end of the gym and touched the wall. As they touched, they used the wall to push off to give themselves extra momentum for their return down the gym. The next runners had their hands up ready to be tagged. As soon as the first runners flew past them, touching their hands, the next runners flew away up the length of the gym.

Toby waited.

Nathan was the fastest of the team leaders, and had given Toby's team a good lead, which the next two runners in line had held, and which the fourth runner had actually increased. The gym was a riot of shouting, encouraging, urging voices.

The fourth runner pounded back toward Toby. Casually, Toby held out his hand, waist high. Behind him, he heard Nathan, forgetting in his excitement his earlier scorn, shout, "Go, Toby!"

Toby turned to Nathan. "Are you serious?"

He took three short running steps up the gym, to put himself clear of his line and in full view of the rest of the class. He said to himself, *This is what I think of the race, and of the gym, and of all of you keeners.*

Toby stopped. He put his hands in his pockets. He strolled casually to the end of the gym. He turned around and waggled his hips so that his bum touched the back wall as if he was doing the bump dance with it. He sauntered back toward the line, his hands still deep in his pockets. By this time, all the other teams had finished, and he was the only one out on the gym floor.

Ms. Watkins had one hand on her hip and was pointing at Toby with the other: "Go straight to the principal's office, Toby Morton."

2

Not a Good Day

Toby, bored, sat outside the principal's office, gazing around. A line of kindergarten students appeared at the end of the long, white tiled hallway. He watched their slow approach as they meandered between the pink and purple walls, heads bobbing and turning as their eyes were irresistibly drawn to every distraction, a teacher's voice raised in a classroom here, student paintings of turkeys on the wall there, a burst of laughter from a classroom behind them.

Looking from the kindergarten students to the white tiles beneath their feet, Toby shook his head. Really, white tiles! Perfect for showing up the scuff marks and the dirt left behind by the two hundred pairs of student feet passing back and forth along the hallway every day. *Good choice, Mr. School Architect*, he thought.

Toby knew the white tiles and the pink and purple walls were supposed to make the old school more attractive. But all they did was make him feel as if he was spending his days inside a raspberry cheesecake ice cream.

The line of kindergarten students marched closer. They were on their way to the lunch room. They all carried their lunch box in one hand with the index finger of the other held to their lips. The leading student slowed, turned her head to look curiously at Toby, and, without moving her finger from her lips, gravely waved her little finger on the same hand at him. Toby lifted one hand and wiggled his fingers in return. As the leading student resumed walking, the next student paused, looked, and waved one little finger. Toby waved back again, and continued waving as each passing student copied the actions of the one in front.

"Are you guys on remote control, or what?" Toby asked.

He knew the answer.

The students were under remote control, the remarkable remote control of their teacher, Miss Little. Toby remembered being under the same control when he was in her kindergarten class. Sure enough, Miss Little, tall and blonde and thin, with her big round glasses perched precariously on the end of her nose, marched at the end of the line. She, too, looked curiously at Toby. She didn't wave, but she smiled and shook her head, sympathetically and sorrowfully.

"What is it this time, Toby?" she whispered, pushing her glasses up her nose as she peered down at him. Whenever Miss Little started to speak, she pushed back her glasses so that she could gaze at her listener with her big blue eyes. Then, as she spoke, the glasses slipped down to their usual fascinating, precarious position at the end of her nose. She always smiled as she spoke. Looking up at her, Toby remembered how much he'd enjoyed being in kindergarten with Miss Little. He remembered the freshness and the newness of it, before he had to begin each new year with the baggage of the old weighing heavily on him. He remembered Miss Little speaking sharply to him quite often in kindergarten, but he also remembered her smile, and her warm voice, which repeated, "What is it this time, Toby?"

Before Toby could answer, the door of the principal's office opened. Miss Little quickly straightened up and followed her students. Mr. Lowry, the principal, sternly watched Miss Little and her charges until they were out of sight around the corner of the hallway. Then he turned his attention to Toby.

"Would you like to tell me why you're here, or shall I just wait for the discipline report?" Mr. Lowry demanded.

Toby shrugged. "Don't care."

"That seems obvious. I have more discipline reports on you than on any other student in the school, and your marks are no better than your behaviour. I'll remind you that tomorrow's field day is the last day of the school year. If you want to help your school record, you'll demonstrate a change in attitude." Mr. Lowry concluded, threateningly, "I'll be watching you carefully tomorrow during field day."

* * *

June at Brunswick Valley School was usually quite a happy time, even for Toby. He liked how the boring routine of school was broken up by trips — "educational visits," as the teachers liked to call them — to the candy factory in Pleasant Harbour, the aquatic centre in Shanklin Bay, the waterfowl park in Westfield Ridge. He liked watching the leaves emerge on the trees that lined the streets of the little southern New Brunswick town where he lived, and he liked watching the lupins flower beside the river that ran through the middle of the town.

The only thing he didn't like about June was Field Day, when all the students took turns trying different sports, the usual ones like running and jumping and throwing, and silly ones like the three-legged race, the running backwards race and the shoe toss. It didn't matter what the event was, Toby failed miserably at it, and hated it.

Toby's class started the day on the back field. Their first event was the shoe toss. The students sat in a circle, facing outwards. Toby, daydreaming moodily as he sat, stared across the tufty grass at the dull brick of the old school. It was as ugly from the back as it was from the front. They could dress it up as much as they liked on the inside — and they had tried, he had to admit, with the white tiles and the pink and purple walls — but it would always be ugly on the outside. It was just a big brick box. It wouldn't have been so bad if they'd left the old windows, but most of them had been filled in. Toby could see their shapes outlined by the newer bricks. It was to save heat, he knew, but it increased the forbidding brickiness of the exterior. The doors and windows had been painted a vivid green the previous summer, and a new sign announcing Brunswick Valley School had been erected. Toby quite liked the new sign, with its gold lettering on a green background. But it was like the parents who tried to dress younger than they were, fathers with baggy carpenter pants and mothers with bare midriffs. Toby wanted to say to them, *You're old. You're over twenty. Face up to it. There's nothing you can do about it.* He wanted to say the same to the school. A plaque in the brick by the main door said "1951." It was old and there was nothing anyone could do about it.

Toby was reflecting that brick must have been popular in 1951, to have been used so much, when his daydream was interrupted by Mrs. Johnson, their homeroom teacher, calling, "Shoes — off!" The game had started.

The students removed their shoes. Toby reached one foot, with difficulty, grasped his shoe, and began to lever his foot out. He rested for a moment, then reached for his other foot.

"Shoes — in the circle!" Mrs. Johnson ordered.

The children tossed their shoes over their heads into the circle. Toby worked his second foot loose, his fingers reaching, grasping and slipping.

"Toby, dear, will you hurry, please?" Mrs. Johnson urged. She called all the students "dear," and treated them all, regardless of age, as if they were her grandchildren. She was small and thin, with curly grey hair and fingers so bent and stiff with arthritis that she could hardly hold a pencil. She always wore a dark blue cardigan and a tartan dress, with brown tights and black lace-up shoes. The students called her Granny Johnson.

"I'm trying," Toby muttered. He was beginning to sweat with the effort of reaching and pulling at his shoe. No matter how he sat, his stomach seemed to get in the way of his efforts. At last his foot was free. He paused to catch his breath, then threw his shoes into the circle.

"Ready?" Mrs. Johnson asked.

The students nodded eagerly, sneaking glances over their shoulders at the scattered pile of shoes behind them.

"*Shoes!*" Mrs. Johnson called.

The students leaped to their feet, shrieking with excitement, and scrambled among the shoes, scrabbling, grabbing and digging through them to find their own. Toby rolled onto all fours and pushed himself to his feet. By the time he started into the circle, the other students already had one or two of their shoes back on, and were moving back to their starting places, some hopping and lurching and pulling on shoes as they moved.

Only two shoes, Toby's, were left in the middle, lying wide apart. Toby lowered himself heavily to the ground, pulled on his first shoe, and, without bothering to tie it, rolled again to all fours and pushed himself to his feet. Now all the other students were sitting back in the circle, shoes replaced, and as Toby lowered himself to the ground beside his second shoe, Nathan began to chant, softly, "Toby, Toby." Others joined in, clapping with the rhythm of the chant: "Toby, Toby." Mrs. Johnson said, "Now, children," but the chanting and clapping swelled louder and louder as Toby pulled on his second shoe, pushed himself to his feet, plunged toward the circle — and stomped on through it.

He heard Mrs. Johnson plead, "Toby, dear, come back and take your place in the circle, please." Toby kept going. At the corner of the school he stopped and looked back. The chanting and clapping had faltered and stopped with his defiance of Mrs. Johnson. She repeated her request: "Toby, please come back this minute and take your place in the circle." Toby moved out of sight, slinking along the side of the school until he reached the dumpster. He glanced around, and, seeing no-one, slipped behind it.

Toby spent the rest of the morning behind the dumpster, until the smell of hot dogs was so enticing that he had to emerge. On Field Day the parents barbecued hot dogs for the students, and at the front of the school he found the children lined up around tables and barbecues where the parents were busy cooking. He slipped into one of the lines. He ate his hot dog, with ketchup, mustard and relish, as quickly as he could, and slipped into the line up at one of the other barbecues. He was taking the first bite of his fourth hot dog when he noticed Mrs. Johnson pointing him out to the principal, who crooked a beckoning finger in Toby's direction. Toby stuffed the rest of the hot dog into his mouth and walked slowly to where Mr. Lowry and Mrs. Johnson waited, stern faced.

"What have you been doing?" Mr. Lowry demanded.

Toby swallowed and said, "Eating hot dogs."

"I mean what were you doing before you ate your hot dogs?"

Toby thought for a moment, and said, "Putting ketchup and mustard and relish on hot dogs."

Mrs. Johnson shook her head and said, "That's not the way to talk to the principal, Toby, dear."

Mr. Lowry held up his hand to her and leaned forward in Toby's direction with his hands on his hips. Mr. Lowry wasn't especially tall, but he looked taller than he was because he had a big, square head, which was distinguished by two circles of hair, one fringing the top of his otherwise bald head, and the other his mouth, where his droopy moustache merged with a little beard.

"I mean," said Mr. Lowry, "what have you been doing since you ran away from class?"

"I didn't run away from class."

"What did you do, then?"

"I walked away from class."

"Well where have you been since you walked away from class?"

"Behind the dumpster."

"Why?"

"I like it behind the dumpster."

Mr. Lowry bent even closer to Toby. "I hope you like sitting outside my office as much as you like sitting behind the dumpster, because that's where you'll be spending the rest of the day. It's time you learned that fresh air and exercise are good for you."

* * *

At the end of the day, Mrs. Johnson called Toby back as he was going for the bus.

"Toby, could you wait a moment, please? I need to talk to you."

"I've got to get my bus."

"And I said you are to wait a moment, dear. Please do as you're told without arguing about it."

She shook her head. Toby could always tell when Mrs. Johnson was getting upset because she shook her head and her voice grew whiny. She passed him a school envelope and said, in a whiny voice, "This letter contains an important message. I've been trying to telephone your mother, but I can't get through."

"That's probably because the phone's been cut off again. Ma keeps forgetting to pay the bill."

"So I want you to take this home and be sure to give it to your mother, and tell her I tried to call."

"What's it say?"

"That's nothing to do with you, dear. You can go now." She turned away, then turned back. "Well ... it is to do with you, but your mother should hear the news first, and she'll tell you."

"I can't wait," said Toby, and went for his bus.

Once on the bus, he examined the letter. On the envelope it said, "Mrs. Morton. Private and Confidential." He opened it and read:

> Dear Mrs. Morton,
>
> I'm sorry to say that Toby has failed this school year, not because he cannot do the work for grade six, but because he has chosen not to do it. In short, his laziness means he will repeat grade six next year.
>
> The only way the school will advance him to grade seven will be his successful completion of summer school.

The letter was signed by Mr. Lowry and Mrs. Johnson.

Toby looked out of the bus window, his head carefully turned away from the other students, and watched the woods and fields go by, blurred by his brimming tears. It wasn't fair. They should have told him before. He would have done enough work to get through grade six. It wasn't his fault the work was so boring it wasn't worth doing.

When he arrived home his mother was lying on the couch dipping into a bag of assorted candies while she watched a soap opera. She smiled a dimpled smile up at him and said, "Hi, lovey. Have a snack." Her face was round and shining. Everyone said his mother had a lovely smile, and Toby often wondered whether it would still be a lovely smile if it wasn't such a chubby smile. She held the candies out to him. He helped himself, looking down at her metallic blonde hair, and said, "Your roots are showing, Ma."

"You don't need to tell me. What have you got there?"

"A letter from school — for you. You won't like it."

When his mother read the letter, she said, "Well I guess it's summer school for you. That — or you're in grade six again. What do you want to do?"

"Summer school, I suppose," he said, seeing the lazy, warm days of summer slipping away from him.

3

Summer Prison

Summer school (summer prison, Toby called it) was a disaster from the very first day. There were a dozen students there and they all seemed very anxious to be successful. The summer school teacher, Mrs. Langmaid, who Toby thought should have retired about a hundred years ago, said at the start of the first class, "Now, boys and girls, we're here to work very hard together so that we can get our grades up where they should be. Are you all ready to work really hard for me?"

She smiled around at the little group. Toby raised his hand.

"Toby Morton, isn't it? What is it, Toby?"

"May I go to the washroom?"

"Well, we've only just started class. You may go, but tomorrow just make sure you go before we start, dear. We don't want to waste time, do we?"

Toby left the classroom, walked past the washroom, and went outside. He sat behind the garbage dumpster and closed his eyes. He was angry and bitter at the school for failing him. An hour later, bored and tired of the smell of rotting garbage, he sauntered back to the classroom. All the students had their heads down, filling in worksheets of some kind.

"Toby, you've been in the washroom an awfully long time, dear. What have you been doing all this time?"

"What do you usually do in the washroom? Do you want a description?"

Mrs. Langmaid's lips tightened, and from then on she ignored him. His week-one report read, *Toby is doing very little work.* (He'd managed one spelling worksheet and half a mathematics worksheet.) His week-two report said, *Toby has done even less work than last week.* (He'd filled in three out of twenty blanks on a grammar worksheet.) Week three: *There is no point in Toby being here if he refuses to work.* (He'd passed in six worksheets a day, all of them blank, and had spent most of his time behind the dumpster.) At the end of Monday at the beginning of week four, Mrs. Langmaid said, "You haven't done one stroke of work, Toby. Please don't come back."

"Thank you," said Toby.

* * *

When he arrived home, his friend Amy was in the road skipping. Toby and his mother lived with his stepfather on a dead-end road which was also a hill. It was outside the town and there were fields and woods all around. Toby lived halfway down the hill, and Amy and her mother lived at the bottom in the only other house on the hill. Amy, who was two years younger than Toby, was home schooled by her mother.

"How was summer school today?" Amy asked.

"I quit."

"Oh, Toby. Why didn't you just do the work? You know you can do it."

"It wasn't work. It was worksheets. They shouldn't be called worksheets. They should be called keeping-kids-quiet-sheets."

"Oh, Toby," Amy said again.

* * *

Toby spent the rest of the summer holidays lonely and bored. He rose late, after his mother and Conrad, his stepfather, had gone to work. He watched the morning television shows as his breakfast snacking merged with his lunchtime snacking. In the afternoons, he walked from the couch to the road, where he stopped and gazed up and down the hill. Amy and her mother had gone away to visit relatives for the rest of the summer, and with his mother and stepfather gone during the day, Toby was alone on the hill.

Often, he sauntered down to Amy's house and leaned on the front gate, admiring the flowers, which crowded the path leading to the front door. He liked Amy's yard more than his own, where there was nothing to do now that he'd outgrown playing in Conrad's old half-ton. It sat on its rims beside the house, without doors or lights or an engine or anything else that Conrad could remove and use somewhere else. The rest of Toby's yard was either soft dirt or hard dirt, the soft dirt where Conrad grew his potatoes and carrots, the rest of the yard hard dirt. There was no hard dirt in Amy's yard. The soft dirt was filled with flowers and vegetables, and the rest of the yard was grass with stone paths winding through it. Toby liked to stroll up the path to the front door and then around the house to the back garden, where he sat contentedly among the flowers and vegetables. Often he dozed through the afternoon there, his mind a fuzzy blank as he pushed away thoughts of school, and of the humiliation of repeating grade six.

4

Nothing Changes

It was the first day of the new school year at Brunswick Valley School, and Toby had lots on his mind. Like failing last year, and like failing summer school. Like being in the same grade again — the same grade six, but this time with a bunch of kids barely out of grade five. They would all be a year younger than him and would look at him with a mixture of pity and disgust when he first entered the classroom.

And who could blame them? How else should they react to a loser like him? Toby pitied himself too, for his laziness, for his poor marks in school, for his rudeness, for his weight and size. He felt disgusted. The only thing he liked about himself was being able to make people laugh, but often he wasn't sure whether people were laughing at his wisecracks or at him.

The thought of repeating grade six had hung like a black cloud over his summer, and it nearly made him run from the bus stop on this first morning of the new school year. In fact he might have done so, had he not seen Amy, just back from visiting her relatives, watching him from her front window, waving and smiling encouragingly.

Toby's was one of the furthest stops on the bus route, and when he got on there were only two other students on board, both going to the high school. He sat halfway back and stared out the window, keeping his eyes fixed there at each stop as more students got on. Some were his classmates from last year, and they looked at him curiously. Word had got around about his failing summer school, and they knew he wouldn't be with them this year in grade seven. Brunswick Valley School was an elementary school that went to grade eight, and the grade sevens were among the oldest kids in the school, the ones the other kids looked up to the most. Eventually, as the bus filled, a high-school girl sat beside him. He didn't want to be friendly with anyone and was feeling like an outcast. One of his former classmates, Tyson, with whom he'd spent a few morning breaks last year, offered, "Hi, Toby," but Toby said, "Just leave me alone." He was grateful that the high-school girl shielded him from the others his age.

When the bus stopped at the school, he slunk off and made himself as invisible as he could, lurking beside his old friend the garbage dumpster, from where he could survey the gravelled school yard.

* * *

The older students stood in groups whose numbers ebbed and flowed as they moved excitedly from one cluster to another. The younger children either darted around with no apparent aim except to get in the way of as many of the older students as possible, or else they ran from the slides to the monkey bars to the rope ladders in the far corner of the playground, hardly stopping to play on any piece of equipment.

Seeing the teacher on duty looking the other way, Toby slipped into school and made it to the washroom without being challenged. As he entered, he caught a glimpse of himself in the mirror. He looked away quickly, but not quickly enough. He'd seen what he didn't want to see.

Himself.

Steeling himself, he looked back.

Well, the hair was alright, blonde, cropped close, and spiky. But his close-set eyes looked sunken and narrow because of the puffiness of the face surrounding them. His mouth, he had to admit, looked pouty, his thin lips drawn down into a permanent sulk.

Then his gaze travelled downward to his body, and stopped.

Yes. He was big, and he hated it, and he was ashamed of it. The sight of his body reflected in the mirror filled him with disgust.

He addressed his reflection: *No wonder you don't have any friends. Who'd want to be friends with a pathetic blob like you?*

Looking out of the window at the crowded playground, he stuffed his hands into his pockets. His fingers closed on a comfortingly familiar shape. He pulled out a chocolate bar, unwrapped it, nibbled slowly on it while watching, and hating, the social scene outside, the chatting, the laughing, the friendships.

The bell rang like a sick alarm clock, starting with a sort of gurgle, then changing to a high-pitched whine, which lasted for about five seconds before lapsing back, through its strangled gurgle, into silence.

Toby watched the students file obediently into school. He slipped out of the washroom. The hallway was filled with children, jostling and pushing one other, taking books out of bookbags, taking off coats, changing outside shoes for inside shoes, hanging up bookbags, checking lunch money, joking, gossiping, accusing, wisecracking.

At the end of the crowded hallway he could see last year's classmates heading upstairs to the grade seven classrooms. Some of them looked at him, but he didn't know whether it was with sympathy or scorn. Scorn, most likely, he guessed. Of course he didn't care about school, and he didn't care what class he was in. All the same, he confessed to himself, he would have preferred to be with his familiar class, and not to have felt so outcast, a grade seven student in grade six. He dreaded walking into his new classroom, where all the new grade six students would know that he had failed; would look at him curiously; would shake their heads, thinking: What a loser.

In order to delay that moment as long as possible he made a show of hanging his bookbag on one of the pegs outside his classroom, and of checking what was inside it to see what he would need to take into class. In fact there was nothing inside it except what his mother had put there for his morning snack, two chocolate bars, and for his lunch, a bag of chips. He was supposed to have brought scribblers and pencils and binders according to the list the school had sent out at the end of the previous year. But he hadn't bothered to tell his mother. He didn't want to be like the students around him who were excitedly bringing out packets of sharpened pencils and bundles of brand new scribblers.

The bell rang a second dreary, wheezy command, and the hallway quickly became silent and empty. Toby sat on the bench under the coat rack and pretended he was changing into his indoor shoes, although he didn't have any indoor shoes to change into. He felt less conspicuous sitting down with jackets and coats hanging around him. He was surprised to find he'd taken out one of the bars meant for his morning snack, and had eaten it, and had the empty wrapping paper in his hand. He crumpled it up and threw it behind him.

He always felt like laughing at the bell, except that he hated it so much, almost as much as he hated the gym. He hated the bell for its bossiness. He didn't like being bossed around at the best of times, but it was worse when you were being bossed around by something not even alive. He hated it for the power it seemed to have over everyone, as if it was the bell that ran the school, and not the people, like the teachers, and the janitors, and the secretary.

And the principal, who suddenly emerged from his office. Whenever the bell rang, the students and the teachers hurried into their classrooms and closed their doors, while Mr. Lowry opened his door and came out into the hallway, as if he was compelled by the bell to move in the opposite direction to the students and the teachers.

Toby should have been prepared for this; he'd seen it so often before as he lagged behind everyone after the bell. He shrunk back among the coats, hoping to make himself invisible, but it was too late.

He heard, *"Toby Morton!"*

Mr. Lowry strode up the hallway and loomed over Toby.

"Toby Morton, you spent last year avoiding work as much as possible. Now here you are skulking in the hallway doing exactly the same thing on the first day of the new year. You're already spending another year in grade six, and if this sort of thing continues I can promise you that you'll be spending a third year in grade six. What do you have to say for yourself?"

Toby, from his sitting position, looked up at Mr. Lowry, towering above him, and said the first words that came into his head: "I can see right up your nose."

"What?" said the principal.

"I can see right up your nose. I can see lots of little whiskers and things," Toby elaborated.

The principal went very, very red.

Through clenched teeth, pointing to the classroom with a shaking finger, he said, "Toby Morton, get yourself into class right now."

Toby decided it was probably time to go to class. He heaved himself up, sauntered deliberately slowly past Mr. Lowry and opened the classroom door. After the pink and purple of the hallway, the cream walls of the classroom looked bright, especially with the white tiled floor and the sun shining through the windows that lined one side of the room. The walls were bare except for a banner hung across the top of the blackboard stating "Doing Your Best Is The Best You Can Do." The students were sitting silently at their desks. They turned and looked at Toby, but no-one spoke. There was no teacher in sight.

Daphne, a frail, freckle-faced girl whom Toby remembered from grade five the previous year, whispered, "Sit down, Toby."

He remembered Daphne because last year she'd often passed him in the hallway, while he was waiting to see the principal and she was running errands for her teacher. She'd always smiled shyly and sympathetically at him as she passed. He'd liked that, although he'd never spoken to her.

"Where am I supposed to sit?" he asked.

"Our names are on our desks. Look." She pointed to a name tag stuck at the top of her desk. "The teacher's voice came over the intercom and told us he was talking to a parent, and would be here soon. He said we were to sit still and silent until he came."

Toby looked up and down the rows of desks. There was one empty place near the back of the class. He read "Toby Morton" on the name tag, and sat down. Sitting nearby he saw Silas, Jason and Nicholas, whom he remembered from last year because they'd often been waiting at the same time as him to see Mr. Lowry, and had teased him cruelly and unmercifully while they waited with him.

He heard Silas say to Jason and Nicholas in a fake whisper loud enough for the whole class, "Do you think that chair's going to hold him, guys?"

Jason whispered back, loudly, "It should hold him. They knew it was going to be Toby's chair, so they made the legs twice as thick as usual, so it wouldn't break when he sat down."

Toby put his arms on his desk, lowered his head and closed his eyes. It was starting already, the teasing, just like last year, just like the year before, just like every year.

"I guess he can't hear us," said Nicholas.

"Yeah. His ears are too clogged up with fat, probably," said Jason, and laughed. Some of the other students did, too.

Daphne said, in a quavering voice, "Shut up, you guys. Leave him alone."

Toby kept his head down and his eyes closed.

"He must be one of a kind," Jason went on. "You don't often see human beings that big."

Silas added, "He's one of a kind alright — except for his mom. She's about as big as he is."

A few other students snickered again. Toby rose slowly from his desk. He didn't always get on famously with his mother, and it was true, she was big, like him, but he knew it would be wrong for him to let them talk about her like that. He walked slowly toward Silas.

"Look out," said Jason. "He's going to roll on you and squash you."

Toby took Silas' arm, heaved him easily out of his desk and threw him to the floor like a rag doll. He'd just grabbed hold of Jason when the door opened and a voice snapped, "Toby. Let go. Sit down. Silas, pick yourself up and sit down, too."

The newcomer strode to the teacher's desk at the front of the room. He was tall, with fair hair that flopped over his eyes in the front, and was tied in a ponytail at the back. He looked athletic, not in a muscular way, but in a wiry, fit-looking way.

"I'm John Walker. That's Mr. Walker to you. I'm your homeroom teacher for this year. My instructions to you over the intercom were to find your desks and to sit silently until I arrived. Four of you have chosen to ignore me, and I'll be speaking to the four of you while you stay in at recess. I do not expect to be disobeyed again. Now, take out a new scribbler. Take out your mathematics books. Open them at page four. Let's talk about fractions."

The next two hours passed in a slow-motion haze of books taken out, books put away, books opened, books closed, names and dates written at the top of pages, names written on labels in the front of books. Every now and then Mr. Walker's voice echoed through the fog in Toby's brain.

"Toby, open your book, please."

"That's page fifty-two, Toby."

"Get something written down, please, Toby."

He borrowed a few pieces of loose-leaf from Daphne. He wrote his name at the top of some of them, and sometimes he wrote a few words, or a few figures, but mostly he did nothing. He saw Mr. Walker watching him several times, but he wasn't going to worry about that.

When the bell wheezed for recess, Mr. Walker said, "You're dismissed, except for those of you who disobeyed me earlier. Silas, Jason, Nicholas, you'll report for detention. Toby, you'll spend recess in here with me."

"Sounds cosy," said Toby.

The students paused in their exit, curious to see how their new teacher would respond to Toby's rudeness. Mr. Walker, his hands in his pockets, strolled to Toby's desk, looked hard at him, then turned suddenly and snapped at the other students, "I said you're dismissed."

They scurried out.

Toby leaned back in his desk, his hands behind his head, his legs stretched out.

When the other students had gone, Mr. Walker said, "Toby, I know what happened. I was listening on the intercom, making sure the class was quiet until I'd dealt with a parent. I heard them teasing you, and I don't blame you for being upset. But getting mad at them and fighting them is not the answer."

"Okay," said Toby. "Can I go now?"

Mr. Walker took a deep breath.

"I can help you handle the teasing."

"Yeah. I know. Like, ignore it and it'll stop. And like, tell a teacher, and the teacher will tell them to stop. Right?"

"They're both good strategies, yes."

"And neither of them work. Ignore it, and they do it even more. Tell a teacher, and the teacher says — guess what — ignore it, and it'll stop."

"There are other things you can do. They'd be harder, and they'd take longer to accomplish, but I guarantee they'd finish the teasing."

"You're going to wave a magic wand and turn me into Superman, right?"

Mr. Walker burst out laughing. "I'm trying to help, you know."

"You can help by just leaving me alone."

Without being dismissed, Toby rose and headed for the door.

He walked slowly, to give Mr. Walker time to call him back, and to tell him to stay. At the door, Toby looked back, and met Mr. Walker's eyes still on him. Mr. Walker said nothing.

I knew it, Toby thought, leaving the room. He doesn't even care enough to tell me not to walk out on him.

Toby went to his bookbag, took out his recess bag of chips, and ambled slowly out for recess, munching on them.

5

Not a Runner

By the third week of October, Toby's work amounted to one and a half spelling exercises completed, two pages of mathematics exercises attempted (most of them wrong), five pages of the class novel read, and one page written in his daily journal. In addition, he had done his homework once (with Amy's help), and had made Mr. Walker smile at least once a day, and laugh out loud at his wisecracks three times.

Teasing incidents amounted to Silas, Jason and Nicholas calling him names almost every day as they stood in line behind him in the cafeteria; Nicholas refusing to have him on his team for a chasing game in gym until forced to by Ms. Watkins; all three boys, Silas, Jason and Nicholas, cornering him in the playground and singing a song they'd all learned in grade one, "Hector the Happy Hippo," but with the words changed to "Toby the Happy Hippo," and then running away laughing; and one foot stuck out by Silas tripping Toby as he walked between the seats to his desk before class, and Nicholas commenting, "I'm not surprised you find it hard to stand up, having to carry all that weight around with you."

Things he felt good about amounted to Daphne saying to Silas, Jason and Nicholas, at least once a week, in her tremulous voice, "Leave him alone, you guys;" Miss Little smiling at him, twice, when she passed him waiting to see Mr. Lowry, as she followed her kindergarten students; and — secretly deep down — Mr. Walker's patience with his lack of work. To Toby's surprise, Mr. Walker's patience was making him feel guilty, and he'd begun to wonder whether, perhaps, he should get more work done.

Three times Mr. Walker had asked Toby to stay behind at recess in order to chide him, gently, for not getting his work done. The last time, he'd asked, "Why didn't you do your homework last night, again?"

"I was busy," Toby lied.

"Doing what?"

"I was busy not doing my homework."

"Toby, listen to me. You have to work. You cannot get through school, or life, without working. You were supposed to be writing in your journal this morning, and look — you've done one page, in eight weeks. That makes on average ... let me see ... about half a line, or six words, a day."

"No wonder I'm so tired. I'm overdoing it," said Toby.

Mr. Walker shook his head, trying not to smile. "I wish you were as quick with your work as you are with your wisecracks."

* * *

Just before recess one Friday, Mr. Walker announced to the class: "I'm going to start a cross-country running club. We'll meet and run after school one day a week, and we'll have meets — races, that means — with other schools. The club will be for anyone in grade five, six, seven or eight. I'm hoping some of you might like to take up cross-country running."

Jason put his hand up. "Is cross-country running where you run across fields, and through the woods, instead of round a track?" he asked.

"That's right," said Mr. Walker. "And sometimes you run through town. It depends on how the course is laid out."

Daphne was next with her hand up. "How far do you have to run?" she asked, in her nervous voice.

"The course for your age is usually about five kilometres, but that doesn't necessarily mean you have to run all the way, especially when you're just beginning the sport. You can walk part of the way if you need to."

"It sounds far," said Daphne, wistfully. "I'd sort of like to try it, but I don't think I could go all that way."

"You could — with training," Mr. Walker assured her, smiling.

Silas asked, "Are you a cross-country running expert, or something?"

"No, not an expert. I just love to run. Usually I run between ten and fifteen kilometres every evening, but since I've been teaching here, I've been so busy I haven't had time to run at all. But I decided to start again, and that made me think, perhaps I'd start a cross-country running club. Well, does anyone think they'd like to run?"

Silas, Nicholas and Jason raised their hands immediately. Daphne put her hand halfway up, lowered it quickly, looked around, and raised it halfway again. Silas guffawed, but stopped when Mr. Walker glared at him. Slowly, Daphne raised her hand all the way.

"Good for you, Daphne, and for you, guys. Anyone else?" The students looked around, to see if anyone else raised a hand. Mr. Walker went on, "Toby, how about giving it a try? Why don't you run?"

All the students laughed, except Daphne.

"The only thing I run for is food," Toby retorted, and the class laughed again, but Toby wasn't sure whether it was at his wisecrack, or at the thought of him running.

"If it's cross-country running, how many countries do you have to run across?" Toby wisecracked again, desperately, as the laughter continued. "I suppose you have to take your passport with you, if you're running across countries."

He glared at Mr. Walker, whose face was red.

"Class, that's enough. You're dismissed," Mr. Walker said above the laughter. "Cross-country runners, we'll meet after school next Tuesday for our first practice."

The students filed out. Toby was among the last. As he passed Mr. Walker, the teacher said, quietly, "Toby, I'm sorry. I didn't mean to set you up like that."

"Yeah, right," said Toby.

"I mean it. I wasn't thinking. But I do think, seriously, that you might give it a try."

"Why? To give the runners someone to laugh at? Maybe the other teams would wear themselves out laughing so we'd beat them easily."

"No, of course not. But I think it would be good for you. It would help with your ... with your weight, and that's a problem for you, isn't it? Running would help you get in shape, and then you'd feel better about yourself."

"I feel fine about myself, thank you — except when you set me up to give the other kids a good laugh."

"I apologised for that, and I apologise again. That wasn't my intention, of course. But I do wish — really, I do — that you'd think about running."

Mr. Walker, his face still red, left the room. Toby went back to his desk and slumped in his chair.

He felt foolish, thinking how he'd been warming to Mr. Walker's patience with him, and for thinking that he might work harder for him. He reached in his desk and fingered the chocolate bar he'd brought for his recess snack. He tore the wrapper open, broke off a piece of chocolate, and slipped it into his mouth.

Mr. Walker came back into the room, picked up a pile of exercise books from his desk, and turned to go. Seeing Toby with his mouth full, he said, “I’ve said I’m sorry. It was insensitive of me to ask you in front of the others. But eating isn’t going to help, Toby.”

With his mouth still full, Toby mumbled, “Neither will you apologising and feeling guilty.”

“I still wish you’d try running.”

“The only running I like to do is off at the mouth.”

This time Mr. Walker didn’t laugh at Toby’s wisecrack. “You’re hiding behind wisecracks and food,” he said and left the room.

Toby finished his bar and stayed slumped in his desk until the students came in from recess.

6

Asthma Attack

Amy was playing hopscotch in the road outside her house when the school bus stopped and Toby alighted. He liked getting off the bus at the end of the day and finding Amy there, playing, as she usually was. It was something to look forward to after a bleak day at school.

As soon as she saw Toby, Amy started talking: "Toby, you'll never guess what. Mum and me started a new project today and it's on — guess what, go on, guess — oh alright I'll tell you. It's on ..." Amy paused, breathless, excited and dramatic. "It's on earthworms! You never would have guessed, would you, Toby, would you?"

"You didn't give me a chance. You didn't stop talking long enough for me to get a word in — as usual."

"Oh you silly. You could have guessed if you'd wanted to. Anyway, we're starting this earthworms project and guess what we're going to do, Toby. You'll never guess. We're going to ..."

Toby opened his mouth to suggest Amy and her mother were going to cook and eat earthworms, but Amy rushed on before he could speak.

"Mum and I are going to start a — guess what — a worm bin, for composting."

Toby sat on a rock beside the road, half listening to Amy's excited prattle and half daydreaming. It was a warm fall afternoon. The blueberry fields at the bottom of the hill, and the hay fields across the road, stretched out in patterns of red and gold to the woods in the distance. Toby rarely felt peaceful, but here he did, with Amy still talking at about a thousand words a minute, and with another day of school behind him. He marvelled at how excited Amy always got about the endless projects she did with her mother. He wondered whether he would be excited about learning if, like Amy, he was home schooled by his mother. He couldn't imagine it, though. He couldn't imagine being excited by projects, nor could he imagine his mother home schooling him, especially not with the intensity and imagination with which Amy's mother seemed to home school her.

"Anyway, Toby, tell me, tell me — how was school today? Was it *super* and *stupendous*? Was it? Was it, Toby? Tell me."

"Oh yeah. It was a riot."

"I knew it. I *knew* you'd say that."

"Why d'you ask, then?"

"'Cause I always hope you'll say it was better."

"Some chance."

He looked up at her, still hopscotching as she talked. Amy was Toby's opposite in so many ways. He was fair; she had a dark complexion. His hair was blonde, short and spiky; hers was brown, long and curly. He spoke carefully and slowly; Amy spoke carelessly and quickly, and almost non-stop. He was wide; she was thin, but wiry, and surprisingly strong, as he'd discovered when he playfully grabbed her skipping rope and tried to pull it away early in their friendship. Amy had promptly and easily dispossessed him.

"I don't understand how you can you talk and play hopscotch at the same time," he commented.

"You just do it, silly. Come on. Want to play?"

"Have you got a Game Boy version?"

"Funny. Come on. Come on, Toby. I need someone to play with. I've been on my own all day with no-one to talk to — well, apart from Mum — and no-one to play with. Well, Mum played hopscotch with me this morning but only until it was time for her to do her yoga. Oh. I forgot to tell you. She's going to teach me yoga, too. Isn't that cool? I'll teach you when I know how, shall I? Shall I, Toby? Wouldn't you like to do yoga, Toby? Wouldn't you?"

"Is that where you sit very still and quiet?"

"Yes. That's yoga. It's so cool. Wouldn't you like to do yoga, too?"

"I can't imagine you doing yoga."

"Why not?" Amy stopped hopping, skipping and jumping, and stood over him where he sat, her hands on her hips. "Why not, Toby? Why not?"

"I can't imagine you being quiet long enough."

"Funny, Toby. You're a scream. Come on, play hopscotch with me."

Toby rose slowly from his rock and stood at the start of Amy's chalked hopscotch course. He sighed. He didn't feel like playing hopscotch. He felt like sitting on a rock, day-dreaming and listening to his friend's chatter. But he liked to try and please Amy. In the five years they'd lived side by side in the only houses on the hill, she'd always listened sympathetically to his grumbles about school. She always offered to help him with his homework. ("I wish mum would give me homework," Amy told him. "I'd love to have homework. You're so lucky to have homework." Toby just rolled his eyes and said, "Yeah, right" when she spoke like this.) And never, never, had she teased him. So he liked to try and play with her, to please her, although her games were usually energetic ones.

"Ready, Toby? Ready? Go on, then. Hop."

Toby lumbered forward. Hop, skip, jump. Hop, skip, jump. He paused, resting. Hop, skip, jump. Hop, skip, jump. He rested again, breathing hard. Hop, skip, jump. Hop, skip, ju—His knees buckled and he fell heavily.

"Toby. Oh, Toby. Are you alright, Toby? Are you?"

"'Course I'm alright. I'm just resting."

"Come on. I'll help you up."

Amy offered her hand.

"No. I'll lie here and be a hop, skip and jump obstacle."

As Amy hopped, skipped and jumped around him, Toby lay in the road with his eyes closed, enjoying the warmth of the late afternoon sun on his face. Amy was still talking about her earthworm project.

"And Mum and me, we're going to get some special red worms — I bet you didn't know there were different kinds of worms, did you, Toby? There are over two thousand kinds of earthworms, so there. And a worm has five hearts. I bet you didn't know that either, did you, Toby? And they breathe through their skins. Anyway, we're going to get special red worms and we're going to put them in a special worm bin with shredded newspaper and water and earth and then we can watch them and we can see them lay cocoons and see them hatch and they'll make compost and it'll be really, really exciting and look there's someone running past the top of our hill."

Toby opened his eyes just in time to see Mr. Walker run past the end of their road, at the top of the hill. A moment later, he reappeared, running backwards, like an instant replay. He looked down the hill at Toby, still lying in the road.

"Toby, is that you?"

"Yes, it's me, Toby."

"Are you alright?"

"As alright as I'll ever be."

Jogging on the spot, Mr. Walker called, "Why are you lying on the ground?"

"Same reason as you're on your feet. I like it that way."

Mr. Walker laughed, waved and jogged on out of sight.

"Who was that?" asked Amy.

"That was Mr. Walker."

"Who's Mr. Walker?"

"My homeroom teacher."

"Wow. Your homeroom teacher. How super. You're so lucky to have a homeroom teacher. What's Mr. Walker like, Toby? He seemed nice. He seemed really nice. He's got a craggy face."

"What do you mean, he's got a craggy face?"

"I mean it's like it was carved out of a rock, and it's all strong, and determined. And he's got a *ponytail*. Oh wow. Is he nice? Is he really, really nice? Is he, Toby?"

"He's alright, I suppose." Toby thought back to that afternoon in the classroom, and added, "Except when he goes on about running. Just because he likes running, he thinks everyone should like running."

"What's wrong with running, Toby?"

"Nothing's wrong with running, except telling people they should do it."

Amy stopped her game and put her hands on her hips. She coughed, and looked hard at Toby. "Did Mr. Walker tell you you should run, Toby? Did he?"

Toby sighed, remembering how upset he had been at Mr. Walker. "Sort of."

"Sort of what, Toby?"

"He sort of told me — no, he sort of suggested, not told — he sort of suggested I should join his cross-country running club. He's starting one next week. He likes running; that's why he was running past our road, I guess, because he wants to get back in shape for running. He said he was starting to run again tonight."

"And what did you say?"

"What did I say to what?"

"What did you say when Mr. Walker sort of suggested you join his cross-country running club?"

"I sort of told him no way."

Amy coughed again and said, "Oh, Toby." She resumed hopping and skipping and jumping, stopping to catch her breath and cough in between bursts of activity.

"Well, I got a bit mad," Toby confessed, feeling that somehow Amy was disappointed with him, and finding that, despite himself, he wanted to talk about Mr. Walker's efforts to get him to run. "He said, 'How about you, Toby?' And the other kids laughed." Toby felt his face grow red at the memory.

"Oh, Toby," Amy said again, resting and breathing heavily. She coughed hoarsely, and resumed her game, hopping around Toby, who lay back again with his eyes closed.

"I told Mr. Walker ..."

A familiar sound made him stop and sit up. Amy was bent over, her hands on her knees, gasping and coughing in between short, laboured breaths. Toby had seen this before. Amy was in the grip of an asthma attack. Last time had been at Christmas, when she grew so excited about Toby and his mother and stepfather visiting for supper on Christmas Eve. Amy had worried about it, and been excited by it, for days. It was the first time her mother had invited friends to visit, and Toby and his family were barely in the house before Amy had started gasping and coughing, just like she was now.

"Have you got your puffer?" Toby asked.

Amy shook her head, unable to speak.

"Shall I get it for you? Where is it?"

Between gasps, Amy blurted out, "Puffer ran out ... Mum walked into ... town to drug store ... to renew prescription ... Won't be back ... for ages."

Toby stood awkwardly beside his friend. How should he comfort her? He put his hand tentatively on her shoulder as she bent and coughed.

"What shall I do?"

"Hospital ... I need ... the ambulance."

"I'll call for it. Don't worry. I'll get the ambulance."

He knew Amy had no telephone. He also knew his mother still hadn't paid the telephone bill, which meant they were still cut off. That made the nearest telephone — he forced himself to stop panicking, and to think — that made the nearest telephone at Mrs. Evans' house.

"I'll get help. I'll call the ambulance from Mrs. Evans'. Don't worry."

Amy was now doubled up in the road, gasping more and more desperately. Mrs. Evans lived just over a kilometre away on the road toward town. Toby set off up the hill, running. The first few steps were easy, carrying him past his house. Pictures began to form in his mind as he ran, of his racing to Mrs. Evans' house; of calling the ambulance; of old Mrs. Evans saying something like, "Toby, you ran all that way to help your friend"; of the ambulance arriving (he'd have jogged back to Amy by then) and the ambulance attendants saying, "Who called us? Where did you call from? Well, sir, that was a gallant run to save your friend"; and of Amy saying, "Thank you, Toby. I don't know how you managed to get to the telephone so fast."

But by the time Toby reached the top of the hill, he could hardly breathe. His lungs hurt and his legs felt as if they would buckle beneath him at any moment. He stopped, caught a glimpse of Amy crouching in the road, fighting for breath, and pretended he'd stopped to wave. Then he staggered on, turning in the direction of Mrs. Evans' house. As soon as he was out of sight of Amy, he stopped again. He put his hands on his knees. His chest was pounding so hard he wondered whether his heart would burst through. Toby marvelled at how difficult and painful it had become to breathe. He thought of Amy, in a far worse fight for breath than him, and took three more faltering steps before falling to his knees in the road.

He heard running footsteps behind him. The footsteps slowed, stopped. He felt a hand on his shoulder.

"Toby. Are you alright? What's the matter?"

Mr. Walker squatted beside Toby.

"I've got to get help. Got to telephone from Mrs. Evans' ... Get an ambulance for Amy ..." Toby could hardly find the breath to speak.

"Is Amy the friend you were playing with?"

Toby nodded.

"What is it? Is she hurt?"

"Asthma attack."

"Where is she?"

"In the road back there, down our hill. She's crouched right down."

"Where's the nearest phone?"

"Mrs. Evans' house. Big white house in a field ... That way ... About a kilometre."

"I'll call the ambulance. You go back to Amy. Stay with her. Keep her as quiet as you can."

"I told her I'd get the ambulance."

"I know. But right now she needs your help here. Go on."

With a pat on Toby's shoulder, Mr. Walker was on his way, racing toward Mrs. Evans' house, apparently effortlessly. Toby heaved himself to his feet, and as Mr. Walker disappeared around a bend in the road, still running with amazing speed, Toby dragged himself back down the hill to his stricken friend. As he stumbled and faltered down the hill, he said to himself — I failed, as usual. I messed up. He felt ashamed of himself.

He wanted something to eat, to comfort himself.

7

Not a Hero

The bus driver said, "What's got into you? I've never seen you move so fast."

Toby ignored the jibe and, jumping off the bus at the bottom of the hill, turned up the pathway to Amy's front door. He didn't usually move this fast, he thought, because he wasn't usually worrying about a friend's health. He'd worried all night. The last he'd seen of Amy she was on a stretcher being lifted into the ambulance, which had roared up the hill, siren wailing. Mr. Walker had met the ambulance at Mrs. Evans' and directed it to where Amy and Toby waited. By the time it arrived Amy had been gasping and Toby was panicking: suppose she stopped breathing completely? Each time it seemed that was going to happen, she had drawn a huge, shuddering breath, and then the fight for another gasp of air had started all over again.

"Thanks for looking after your friend," one of the ambulance attendants had said. "You did well."

I could have done better. I could have run and called the ambulance, Toby had thought sadly to himself.

He was still sitting in the road when his mother and stepfather had arrived with Amy's mother, whom they'd picked up as she walked home from the drug store. When Toby told them what had happened, his stepfather took Amy's mother to the hospital, then went straight on to work the night shift. So all evening Toby had worried about Amy. He awoke, still worrying, and then worried all day at school. Now he hurried up the path to Amy's door, hoping for news, barely noticing in his haste the profusion of colour and scent rising from the flowers on each side of the path. Amy's mother opened the door before he knocked, and hugged him.

"Toby. You're our hero."

"No I'm not," Toby mumbled, his face pressed against her flowery dress, his nostrils filled with the smell of patchouli.

He knew it was patchouli because Amy had told him. He liked the smell, but didn't know how to ask what it was, so he had just said, "Your ma smells, doesn't she? What's she smell of?"

"Patchouli."

"Bless you."

"No, silly. Patchouli. It's a herb. Isn't it sensational?"

"It's alright, I suppose, if you like to smell."

Toby adored Amy's mother. He liked not just her smell, but also the long flowered dresses she always wore, her long braided hair, and best of all, her quiet, kind voice.

"Thank you for being Amy's saviour," she said.

"Is she alright?"

"She's asleep. She was awake most of the night with the oxygen mask on her face, then she was so excited at coming home this morning that she still didn't sleep. She knew you'd be calling in when you got home from school. She tried to stay awake, but she dropped off about an hour ago, and I don't want to wake her. I'll tell her you came by. Thank you for being such a good, caring friend yesterday. You really were a hero."

It was the second time that day he'd been called a hero. At recess Miss Little had whispered to him as she passed, "Mr. Walker tells me you were a hero last night. Well done."

Toby refused to let himself believe it. He protested to Amy's mother, "Mr. Walker was the hero, running all that way to telephone for the ambulance."

"Yes, and you were the hero, too, for looking after Amy. She would have been so frightened if she'd been left by herself."

Toby found himself enveloped in a haze of patchouli and flowers as Amy's mother hugged him again. He mumbled into the flowers and patchouli, "I wasn't a hero. I was a failure." But Amy's mother didn't hear.

Toby was still mumbling and grumbling to himself as he walked back through the flower garden to the road: "I should have been the one to run to Mrs. Evans' house and call the ambulance."

He looked up the hill. He could almost see the place where Mr. Walker had found him on his knees, exhausted. It didn't look far. It *wasn't* far. Just up the hill and a few metres toward town. He'd try it again, just to prove he could have run, if he had wanted, to Mrs. Evans' house to call the ambulance. Just to prove he could do it if it happened again.

He broke into an awkward trot. Yes, it was easy. He passed his house and saw his mother watching him curiously from the front window.

Well, perhaps it wasn't exactly easy — but it wasn't *that* difficult.

His chest was starting to heave and hurt, like the day before.

Okay, it was difficult. But still he'd prove he could do it.

Chest heaving, lungs straining, he reached the top of the hill, walking the last few metres. A few more staggering steps and he passed the spot where he'd collapsed the day before. But that was as far as he could go. He felt his legs begin to shake, his throat and lungs begin to ache. He grew dizzy. His legs buckled under him, and he collapsed in the grass beside the road.

He closed his eyes, waiting for the panting hurt in his chest to ease. A picture popped into his mind of a beach that he'd seen in the news the summer before. On the beach was a whale that had swum into a shallow inlet and then been stranded as the tide went out. He'd felt sorry for the whale, lying helpless and exhausted by its efforts to regain the sea.

I'm a whale, thought Toby. Helpless and exhausted. And useless.

Running footsteps disturbed his self-pity. Opening his eyes, he saw Mr. Walker jog past him, saying, "Hi, Toby. Why are you lying down today? Same reason as yesterday — because you like it that way?"

Toby didn't answer. Mr. Walker backpedalled and stopped beside him.

"Toby? What's up? No wisecracks for me today?"

Toby just shook his head. Mr. Walker sat on the grass beside him. Toby sat up and looked at Mr. Walker from the corner of his eye. The teacher's face was red and tiny beads of perspiration glistened in the sun on his forehead and on his upper lip, but he didn't seem to be breathing hard.

"How far have you run?" Toby asked.

"Just out from town. Now I'm heading back."

"How far's that?"

"Only about fifteen kilometres, out and back."

"Aren't you tired?"

"Not really."

"Why do you like running?"

"Because I like to keep in shape."

"Why do you like to keep in shape?"

"Because I like running."

Toby looked at Mr. Walker and raised his eyebrows. Mr. Walker burst out laughing.

"That's better, Toby. It doesn't seem like you not to have something smart to say. You seemed down in school today. Were you worrying about your friend?"

"A bit. But she's okay. She's home now."

"So what else *are* you worrying about?"

Toby shrugged.

They sat in silence, until Mr. Walker said suddenly, "You got further than yesterday."

"What do you mean?"

"I mean you managed to run further today than you did yesterday. That's what you were trying to do, wasn't it?"

Toby looked away, bit his lip, shook his head. Then suddenly he was telling Mr. Walker how he felt he'd let Amy down, and how ashamed he'd felt, not being able to run to Mrs. Evans' to telephone the ambulance.

"I messed up. I was a failure," he insisted.

"You weren't a failure. You rescued her, for heaven's sake. What would have happened if you hadn't been there?"

"What would have happened if you hadn't come along and been able to run and telephone for the ambulance? I'd have been lying here, and Amy would have ... would have ..."

"But Amy's okay. You stayed with her, and that's what she needed — a good friend to keep her calm and look after her. Don't get down on yourself, Toby. You were her hero."

"I'll throw up if anyone else calls me a hero."

"Now you're beginning to sound like the old Toby."

They sat in silence again, until at length Mr. Walker said, "Well, I have to jog on home. I've got some book reports to mark."

He set off, with long, light strides, his arms moving loosely, his ponytail swinging behind him. He turned around and jogged back. "I bet if you joined the cross-country running club you'd be able to run as far as Mrs. Evans' house within a few weeks. And it'd do you good. You'd learn from it — and not just about running. Trust me." Then: "See you, Toby," and he was gone.

8

The Fitness Plan

Toby hadn't told his mother, and he hadn't told his stepfather. He hadn't told Mr. Walker, and he certainly hadn't told any of his classmates. But he thought he might tell Amy, as the bus deposited him at their usual meeting place at the bottom of the hill. He'd thought hard about it, and his plan frightened him. What had decided for him, despite his fear, was the thought of Amy having another asthma attack, and of his having to run for the ambulance, and being unable to do so.

"Amy, you know how I messed up last week when you had the asthma attack," he started. "Well, I've got a plan ..."

Amy, hands on her hips, interrupted him: "For the ten millionth zillionth time, Toby Morton, you didn't mess up. I won't listen to you telling me you messed up, because it isn't true. But I will listen to your plan."

"Well," said Toby, slowly. He stopped, thrust his hands into his pockets and kicked some stones across the road. "Well, I'm going to take up running."

"Oh, Toby, that's a super, sensational idea. It's so exciting it's ... it's ... awe-inspiring. When will you run? After school? On Saturday mornings?"

Toby kicked more stones across the road, and said casually, "I thought I might join Mr. Walker's cross-country —"

Amy interrupted again: "The cross-country running club! That's a stupendous idea, Toby! You're so lucky to have a cross-country running club to join. It'll be so exciting. I'm *thrilled* for you."

Toby had known Amy wouldn't laugh at his plans, but he hadn't expected her to be quite so enthusiastic. He sat on his rock in the road while Amy pranced excitedly around him.

"Oh, Toby, I can see you now, racing across the countryside, hurtling over the fields, zooming through the woods, with your long loping strides eating up the distance and the wind blowing through your hair as you disappear over the horizon with phenomenal speed. Toby, are you alright?"

Toby had fallen backwards and lay flat on the ground. "I'm worn out just listening to you talk about it."

"Oh you silly. Now, Toby, we have to start with a little training." Toby groaned, and Amy said quickly, "No, don't worry, nothing too strenuous. We'll just do a little easy training, to get you warmed up and ready for running."

"I'll lie here and blink. That'd be pretty good exercise, wouldn't it?"

"Oh, Toby. Come on. We'll start now, with some skipping."

"Skipping?" said Toby, in horror. "That means I'll have to stand up *and* swing my arms to make the rope go *and* jump up and down. Can't we start with something simpler?"

"There's nothing simpler than skipping for getting in shape," said Amy firmly. "We'll do salt, mustard, vinegar, pepper." Amy started to skip and chant in rhythm, "Salt, mustard, vinegar, pepper. Salt, mustard, vinegar, pepper ..."

"I've got a better rhyme," said Toby. "Let's do chips, chocolate, hamburger, cola."

They decided to skip to Toby's rhyme. They got as far as 'hamburger,' the second time round, before the rope tangled in Toby's feet.

"Let's try again," said Amy. Toby groaned. They started again, chanting as they skipped: "Chips, chocolate, hamburger, cola. Chips, chocolate, hamburger, cola. Chips, chocolate, hamburger, cola. Chips, chocolate, ham ..."

Toby stopped. He felt the same as when he had run to the top of the hill, and he didn't want to collapse in front of Amy. He sat in the road, and Amy sat beside him.

"I've got another idea for you to get in shape for running, Toby," said Amy, cautiously.

"Oh good. What is it? Pole vaulting? Synchronised swimming? Rhythmic gymnastics?"

"No, silly. It's simpler than that. It's healthy eating."

Toby looked quickly at her. "Why would I want to eat healthy stuff? What's wrong with what I eat?"

"Well some of the things you like to eat, they're not good for being in shape, and they make you ... big, Toby, really they do." Toby looked away. "Come on, Toby. Let's go and ask Mum. She knows about healthy foods and stuff."

Toby knew Amy's mother was particular about what Amy ate. That's what was worrying him. Often she invited Toby to stay for supper when she knew his mother and stepfather were working late. Usually he tried to avoid these invitations and made an excuse to go home, where he foraged in the kitchen until he found chips or fries for supper. All Amy and her mother seemed to eat were bean sprouts and lentils. On the other hand, he thought, watching Amy, who was on her feet again, jumping around and saying, "Come on, Toby, come on. Let's go and find Mum," — on the other hand, perhaps the exuberance and vitality he envied and admired in her, perhaps that came from bean sprouts and lentils. It was the same energy he saw in her mother's briskness around the house and garden, and her walking into town without seeming to think anything of it.

They found Amy's mother in the back garden, digging potatoes. Amy explained that Toby was going to change his diet and eat healthy foods. "Thinking of changing his diet," she corrected herself quickly, as Toby started to protest. Amy's mother planted her spade in the earth, folded her arms and looked thoughtfully at Toby. Her flowered dress merged with the sunflowers and the cosmos growing at the back of the vegetable garden.

"If you're going to change your diet, Toby, the best and easiest way to get started ..."

"I like the sound of easiest," Toby put in, hopefully.

Amy's mother smiled, shook her head, and said gently, "Oh, Toby," sounding just like Amy. Toby could never decide whether Amy was just like her mother, or if her mother was just like Amy.

"Sorry. Didn't mean to interrupt," Toby apologised.

"The best way to start would be for you to choose *not* to eat and drink certain things."

"Like what?" said Toby suspiciously.

"Well ... like chocolate bars, and chips, and french fries, and pop, for a start."

Toby's mouth and eyes opened wide in horror. "No bars? No chips? No fries? No pop? What's left to eat and drink?" he said.

"Oh, lots," said Amy's mother. "And after you've cut out chocolate bars and chips and fries and pop, then we can start getting serious."

"Serious? You can't get much more serious than that."

"You'll see, it'll be easy, and fun. I've got a really nice snack ready now, to start your diet."

"Lentils, I suppose," said Toby, mischievously, and not rudely. He'd never be rude to Amy's mother, or to Amy.

"No, rice crackers," said Amy's mother.

"Oh, wow, super. I love rice crackers," said Amy.

"Look out, stomach," said Toby, and followed them into the kitchen for the first meal of his new diet.

* * *

When Toby walked up the hill to his house after the healthy snack, he found his stepfather, Conrad, stacking wood in the yard.

"Can I help?" he said, feeling a surprising burst of energy and wondering whether it came from the rice crackers. He'd enjoyed the snack, but he wasn't sure whether that was because of the taste, or because of the company of Amy and her mother, who talked and laughed and scurried about as they ate in the kitchen. Being in their house was like being in an endless game of musical chairs. As soon as one sat down after finishing one kitchen job, the other stood up to do something else.

"Suit yourself, big guy," said Conrad.

For fifteen minutes Toby walked between the saw horse and the woodpile carrying armloads of Conrad's freshly cut chunks. By then he was sweating heavily and his legs were shaking again.

He told Conrad, "I'm going to see what's for supper."

Conrad grunted, "Thanks, bud," without stopping his work. To Toby he looked as if he could stack wood forever without tiring. Conrad wasn't tall — in fact he wasn't much taller than Toby — but he was solid, and the flannel shirts he liked to wear with the sleeves rolled up always seemed to fit closely and neatly. He wore his *Flames* ball cap pushed back on his head to allow room for a wave of his thick black hair, Elvis-style, at the front. Toby treasured the rare smiles that sometimes crinkled his stepfather's grey eyes. He looked for one now, but Conrad was busy loading his arms with chunks of wood.

Toby called into the house, "What's for supper, Ma?"

His mother was watching television. "Macaroni and cheese, lovey, but it won't be for a while yet. Conrad's got to go into town first."

"I'll starve."

"Have a bag of chips to keep yourself going."

"Anything else to eat?"

"What's wrong with a bag of chips?"

"Nothing. I just thought I might give them up. Them and pop and stuff."

"You mean, go on a diet, like?" said Mrs. Morton, coming into the kitchen while the advertisements were on.

"Something like that, yeah."

His mother shrieked with laughter and hugged him. "You've been a ball of blubber since the day you were born — like me — and you can diet all you like and you'll be just the same. Take a look at your Ma." Toby knew what she was going to say next. She often said it, patting her stomach after a big meal. "Mrs. Down and Out — that's me. Everything on me is going down and out, from my chin to my tum to my knees." And it was true, so true that she jiggled when she moved, her chin and her stomach and, Toby had noticed, even her knees in the summer when she wore shorts.

Wiping her eyes, she opened the back door and called out to Conrad, "Get this, Con. Our Toby's going on a diet."

Toby stomped outside. As he passed his stepfather, Conrad said quietly, "Not a bad idea, buddy."

Toby went back down to Amy's house and had some more rice crackers with Amy and her mother, who said if Toby kept on snacking just on rice crackers he'd make fast progress.

Amy said, "I know what we'll do. We'll chart your weight loss. We'll weigh you every Saturday morning."

Toby said that would be fine, as long as they weighed him without any clothes or shoes.

Together, Amy and her mother said, "Oh, Toby."

9

Walker's Runners

On the day of the first meeting of the cross-country running club Mr. Walker reminded his class about the practice in the morning. He looked at Toby, but Toby looked down, avoiding his eye. He hadn't told anyone except Amy and her mother about his plan to run.

He'd had two skipping sessions with Amy. They'd made a new skipping rhyme to fit with Toby's diet: "Beans, lentils, sesame, carrots." Their record was six rounds of the rhyme before Toby had to stop. Both times after skipping he'd walked to the top of the hill and back as extra exercise. His leg muscles were stiff and sore, and he felt as if he could hardly lift them.

Mr. Walker said the club would meet after school by the main door, where the run would start. By the time Toby arrived, the other runners had already gathered and were clustered around Mr. Walker outside. Peering through the glass door, Toby saw Silas, Nicholas and Jason in the group and nearly changed his mind, although he was pleased to see Daphne there, too. As he stepped outside the door, all heads turned in his direction, and suddenly he felt embarrassed by his running outfit. The others wore singlets and shorts. All Toby had been able to find was an old T-shirt, a pair of cut-offs, and his dirty, everyday sneakers.

And even though he'd been steeling himself for the surprise and scorn of the more athletic students, he was embarrassed by his size. All the others seemed so … thin, and fit looking. He felt like he didn't belong.

But Daphne turned and beamed at him, and Mr. Walker smiled a welcome, saying, "Glad you could make it, Toby." He didn't seem surprised to see him.

The other runners included a red-haired grade eight student named Derek, whom Mr. Walker called Derek the Red, and who played, and was good at, every sport that existed, and Jillian and Jessica, the twins from grade five who were always grinning and bouncing every time Toby saw them, their identical blonde pony tails bobbing behind them.

As he walked to join the group, he heard Silas say to Nicholas and Jason, "Is this a running club — or a rolling club?" All three laughed but were quickly silenced by a glare from the teacher.

Mr. Walker said, still looking sternly at the three, "The aims of our club are to enjoy running with each other, and to get some good exercise. Our cross-country running club is not about winning or losing; it's about all of you doing the very best you can every time you run. That's called doing your personal best. And …" he said looking at Toby, "you don't have to run all the way. Just walking some of the course will do fine."

"What are we, then?" said Silas. "Walkers or runners?"

Mr. Walker glared at Silas again. "We're a club, a team. We support each other. It doesn't matter whether we're runners or walkers, walkers or runners."

The twins giggled and began to dance up and down, delighted and inspired by the unintended rhythm of Mr. Walker's little speech. "We're runners and walkers, walkers and runners." They made up a clapping routine as they chanted: "Walkers and runners. Runners and walkers."

Despite his nervousness, Toby managed a weak grin: "I guess you could call us Walker's Runners."

Mr. Walker laughed delightedly, and the twins changed their chant to: "We're walkers and runners, and runners and walkers; all together — we're Walker's Runners."

The others joined in, even Silas and his friends.

When they'd finished their chanting and clapping, Mr. Walker explained that there would be one more practice before their first cross-country meet with other schools. He described the practice route, and said, "Now — ready?"

The students leaned forward, one foot before the other, knees bent, arms poised, ready to run. Watching surreptitiously, Toby also leaned forward, put one foot in front of the other, bent his knees and angled his arms.

"Set."

They leaned further forwards. Toby saw the muscles in their back legs tense. He tried to do the same.

"Oh, Toby, I need to go over something with you before you set off, so you wait. Everybody else — Go!"

The little group set off at a brisk trot, Derek leading, followed by Silas, Jason and Nicholas, then the twins, and Daphne in the rear.

Mr. Walker said, "Now, Toby, I just need to ..." He shuffled through some papers in his hand. "Let me see. Where was I? Before you set off, I want to check. Let me see ..." He shuffled through his papers again.

Toby said, "You're trying to spare my feelings, right?"

"What's that?"

"You're pretending you need to talk to me so I won't be embarrassed when the others leave me way behind right at the start, right? This way, I'll start way behind, and it won't look so bad when I finish even further behind."

"I just don't want you to get discouraged the first time out, Toby."

Toby nodded. "I get it." He nodded again. Mr. Walker watched as Daphne, the last of the runners, disappeared from sight. Toby prompted, "Aren't you supposed to say 'go'?"

Mr. Walker said quietly, "Go, Toby."

Toby set off in a kind of lumbering shuffle run, and managed to get around the side of the school, out of sight of Mr. Walker, before he stopped, took a few deep breaths, and then carried on at a walk.

The first part of the course took him around the school. He walked until he came back in sight of Mr. Walker, still standing at the door. He managed to shuffle run past him and out of the school gate onto Brunswick Street before walking again. He walked the length of Brunswick Street quite briskly, then slowed as he joined the next section of the course, the riverside trail. Seeing no-one around, he tried a few running steps, but he was embarrassed and afraid someone would see him running — *a fat kid trying to run*, he told himself mercilessly — and anyway he quickly tired and resorted to walking. He crossed Main Street and entered the Catholic cemetery, the third part of the course. He moved on the footpath through the cemetery in a kind of a dream, and was surprised to find he'd gone all the way through it without being aware of his surroundings. Coming out of his trance, he thought: *Why am I doing this? What's the point?* And he had to remind himself that it was to get in shape in case he needed to run again in an emergency. He limped slowly from the cemetery out on to the Back Road, the final section, and turned toward the school grounds. When at last he stumbled across the school's back field, and around the school to the front entrance, he found only Mr. Walker waiting for him. The rest of the club had long finished their run and had all gone home.

"Sorry to keep you up, waiting for Mr. Lightning here," Toby wisecracked. What he really wanted to say was, "Thank you for waiting for me." But he had to say something to put himself down, the way he always did.

Mr. Walker said, simply, "Well done, Toby. I'm proud of you."

Toby wanted to say thank you again, but instead he quipped, "If you're proud of me for being the worst runner in the club, I hope you'll be just as proud of me for being the worst student in the class."

* * *

The next morning Mr. Walker announced in class: "We're all going to do a project on mammals. You can choose any mammal you like, and you'll research it, and become an expert on it. Finally, you'll do a project on it to present to the class."

Toby, lounging back in his desk, said, "Wow. A project. Be still my heart. How many lines, Mr. Walker?"

"Make that how many pages, Toby."

"Pages? You mean we have to write more than a page?"

"Yes. And include some pictures."

Just before he left the classroom, Mr. Walker said quietly to Toby, "Why don't you stop pretending you're not doing any work, because I know better."

Toby didn't answer. It was true that lately he had been doing some of the work set by Mr. Walker, but he didn't want anyone in class to know. He didn't know why.

While the class waited for Ms. Watkins to arrive for French, Silas said, "Hey, Toby. This should be an easy project for you. You can write about hippos. Want to know why?"

Nicholas and Jason took up their cue: "Looks like one ... Eats like one ... *Is* one. Toby the Happy Hippo. He can write about himself."

They began to sing "Toby the Happy Hippo." Toby had kept his head on his arms, resting on his desk as long as he could, but as they started to sing he raised it and roared at them, "*Shut up!*"

At the same time Ms. Watkins opened the door. "Who is that shouting in that rude manner? Toby? I might have known it was you. Go to the principal's office immediately. I'll buzz the office and tell Mr. Lowry you're on your way."

* * *

At the bottom of the hill after school, in between skipping, Toby told Amy about the project on mammals. "I don't know what to write about."

"Why don't you write about whales? You like whales. Besides, Mum and me did a project on whales, so we can help you. Whales are *the* most *wonderful* creatures, Toby."

"I said it's a project on mammals, not fish."

"A whale *is* a mammal, silly."

"What do you mean? Whales swim in the sea. Whales live in the sea. So whales are fish, right?"

"Wrong. They breathe with lungs, not gills. They have hair, not scales. And they have babies. So whales are mammals. So there, Toby."

Toby was amazed. "Well, what do you know? A whale is a mammal, so I can do my project on whales. That's enough learning for me today. Whew. I'm exhausted. I know what I'll do. I'll copy your project."

"No, you won't, Toby. But Mum and me will help you. Now, on your feet. We have to skip some more before snack time. It's alfalfa cakes today."

* * *

When Toby joined the group for the second cross-country practice, Derek nodded, Daphne smiled, the twins grinned, as usual, and while Silas, Jason and Nicholas didn't greet him, at least they didn't make fun of him, although Toby thought he saw them smirking at something when Mr. Walker wasn't looking.

As they set off at Mr. Walker's "Go," Toby was determined to run further than the previous time. He kept up his shuffle run all the way around the school, but slowed to a walk as he turned into Brunswick Street. By that time the others were disappearing from sight as they joined the riverside walk. Daphne turned to give him an encouraging wave before she, too, disappeared. He tried to run a few more steps, but his lungs and his legs protested too much, and he fell into his usual shuffling walk. Crossing Main Street and entering the cemetery he hoped he might catch a glimpse of Daphne, at least, bringing up the rear, but there was no-one in sight, and he realised that, again, he was a shamefully long way behind the others. He was in one of his moments of mindless day-dreaming, trudging on the cemetery footpath, when suddenly, Amy was with him, talking as she danced around him.

"Toby, I've thought of a fantastic system for you. An amazingly efficient running system. It will improve your running astoundingly."

"I'm not doing much running, actually. I'm mostly just walking," Toby confessed. He added, "Where did you come from, anyway?"

"Mum and me are doing the shopping, and you told me you'd be out running after school, remember? And I guessed you'd be around here somewhere, so I came to join you, to tell you about the running system."

Amy skipped and pranced around him as she talked.

"How can you run and talk at the same time?" he asked.

"Practice," said Amy. "The secret's in the practice. Practice — and having a remarkably super running system." She twirled around him, spinning circles. "Don't you want me to tell you about The System, Toby? It's such a terrifically remarkable system it has capital letters. It's The System."

Toby rolled his eyes. "All right. Tell me about The System."

"It's simple. You run a hundred steps, then you walk a hundred steps."

Toby considered. "Walking a hundred steps sounds okay, but I don't think I could run a hundred."

"We'll start now. We'll walk a hundred steps. Are you ready?"

They counted out one hundred steps as they walked.

"So far, so good," said Amy. "Now — we run a hundred."

With Toby doing his shuffle run, and Amy leaping around him, they counted one hundred running steps.

"Whoa, Toby. Now we walk a hundred," said Amy.

Toby was beyond speech, and almost beyond breathing. But by the time they'd walked another hundred steps, Amy counting every ten aloud, he was ready to do his shuffle run for another hundred steps. They proceeded like this through the cemetery onto the Back Road.

"Gotta go. Gotta meet Mum. See you later," Amy called, and was gone, flying back across the cemetery, as if running was easier for her than walking.

They'd just finished running one hundred steps, and as Toby counted off a hundred walking steps he thought, *I might as well just walk the rest of the way to school.* But when he got to a hundred, he couldn't help breaking into his shuffle run for the next hundred. As he neared the school, still doing The System, Derek passed him, heading home, his backpack on his back, and still running. As he passed, he grinned and gave Toby the thumbs up.

When Toby reached the finishing line, Mr. Walker was trying to hide his surprise at seeing him arrive back not so long after the others this time.

10

Collapse in the Woods

As Conrad swung the truck into the visitors' parking area of St. Croix Middle School, Toby's teeth began to chatter. It was the day of the first meet and Toby was very nervous. The team was to find Mr. Walker on the sports field behind the school, where the run would begin at four o'clock. Conrad had picked Toby up after school and driven him over.

"Ready, big guy?"

Toby gazed unmoving out of the truck window. St. Croix Middle School was surrounded by sub-divisions. It was all pavement in front and all playing field at the back, with the low, sprawling, brick-built school in between. The town of St. Croix was quite big, at least twice the size of Brunswick Valley, and it was as modern as Brunswick Valley was old. There seemed to be hundreds of runners getting out of school buses and parents' cars, which were snaking into the school yard through the rows of houses.

Toby fingered his blue running vest and looked in vain for the same colour in the crowd.

* * *

Mr. Walker had given out new vests to the team the day before. The shirts were light blue, with "Brunswick Valley School" emblazoned on the front. The runners held them up against their chests, eyes wide and bright with quiet pride and excitement. Taking Toby aside, Mr. Walker said awkwardly, "I couldn't find one ... er ... big enough for you, Toby. This is an extra large. Take it home and see what your mom can do to make it ... broader."

Toby couldn't face asking his mother to help, afraid of her laughing again at his efforts to slim down, so after school he went over to Amy's and asked her mother for help. She found some blue material the same colour as the vest and sewed a vent in the back, so neatly that the seam was almost invisible.

"I think that'll do. Now try it on. Give us a fashion show," she said, passing the vest to Toby.

He changed in the kitchen, then burst back into the dining room with a "Ta-daa." Amy and her mother applauded as Toby twirled around like a fashion model. He was beginning to feel better about himself, with his skipping, and his walks to the top of the hill, and the practice runs at school. He suggested going for a run, but Amy said he should save his energy for the meet the next day.

"Are you excited?" Amy's mother asked.

Toby confessed, "Sort of. But I think I'm more scared than excited."

"We'll be thinking of you tomorrow afternoon, won't we, Amy?"

Amy nodded, grinning. Fingering his running vest before their affectionate eyes, and seeing "Brunswick Valley School" written across his chest, he felt proud of belonging to the school, for the first time he could remember.

It was a strange, surprising feeling, but not unpleasant.

In class on the day of the race, Toby couldn't concentrate, and he thought: *Before this running thing started I didn't care whether I concentrated or not. Now I do care, because of the running, but I can't concentrate — because of the running. Is this progress?*

But secretly, he knew it was.

When Mr. Walker was in class, it wasn't too bad. The students were working on their mammal projects. Toby was writing about Why a Whale Is Not a Fish, using some of the notes he'd taken from Amy's project the night before. He was still surprised to find himself so interested in the project. The two times that his attention wandered from his work to worrying about the meet, Mr. Walker said gently, "Need help, Toby?" and he took the hint and got back to work.

In French class he drifted off, thinking about the meet. First, he imagined himself bravely keeping up with his teammates and with the runners from the other schools. Then his daydreaming vision changed. Now he was struggling way behind them, and finishing a distant and embarrassing last. He felt nervousness embracing him in a clammy sweat and forced that image from his mind. He conjured the first image back: of his heroic efforts to keep up with the other runners, of himself crossing the finishing line, of Mr. Walker and Derek and Daphne and the twins cheering him home, chanting his name: "Toby. Toby. Toby ..."

"Toby. Toby! Toby Morton! Will you repeat what I just said to the class?"

He looked around. All the students were looking at him. Ms. Watkins was pointing at him, eyes narrowed.

"I said will you repeat what I just said?" Toby shook his head. "Can you repeat what I just said?" Toby shook his head again. "Just as I thought. Go to the principal's office. I'm sick and tired of your laziness and lack of attention."

Mr. Lowry ranted at Toby: "I'm getting tired of talking to you. You were sent to me yesterday, and now here you are again. I'm ashamed to have you in the school."

Toby recalled how he had felt when he tried on the running vest the night before and thought, bitterly: *Just when I'm getting sort of proud of being in the school, you say you're ashamed of having me here. My mistake. Sorry.*

But when Mr. Lowry asked, "Do you have anything to say?" Toby just shook his head.

As he left the office, Mr. Walker was walking past in the hallway, with Miss Little.

"Are you in trouble, Toby?" Mr. Walker asked.

"Why else would Mr. Lowry want to see me?"

"What happened?"

"I couldn't repeat what Ms. Watkins had said in French class."

"Why not?"

"I guess I was daydreaming."

"What were you daydreaming about?"

Toby shrugged, embarrassed to say, but Mr. Walker guessed, anyway. "Are you worrying about the meet?"

Toby shrugged again.

"What did Mr. Lowry say?"

"He said he was ashamed to have me in the school."

Mr. Walker beckoned Toby to him. "Come here. Listen to me. You've got plenty to be proud of. Don't let anyone tell you anything different. Now, get back to class."

Toby looked at Miss Little, who was nodding in agreement. Stretching out her hand, she formed a loose fist and chucked him gently on the chin.

As Toby set off for his class, looking back he saw Mr. Walker heading into Mr. Lowry's office.

* * *

"Hey, big guy. I said are you ready?" Conrad brought Toby back to the present. "Before you go — here, look, I got something for you." Shyly, Conrad produced a Zellers shopping bag and took out new sneakers and new running shorts.

"I hope these are the right size. They should be. Your ma said they'd fit you. Here, put them on. There's no-one near."

Toby quickly slipped into his new running shorts in the cab of the truck, then tied his new sneakers. The shorts were dark blue, to match the light blue of his vest, and the sneakers had blue and black flashes on the sides. He climbed out of the truck.

"Thanks, Con. How do I look?"

Conrad's eyes crinkled with his smile. "Like a million dollars. Go get 'em. I'll be watching."

Toby joined the throng of runners heading down to the sports field. He saw a cluster of blue shirts and joined his team.

Derek said, "Just give it your best shot, Toby."

Daphne seemed as nervous as Toby and managed only a weak smile as she hopped from one foot to the other. The twins grinned their usual irrepressible grins, while Silas, Jason and Nicholas ignored him. Toby looked at the runners, from St. Croix Middle School, Pleasant Harbour Consolidated School, Keswick Narrows Memorial School and Westfield Ridge Community School, and at his own teammates. They all seemed to be in good shape, except him. He could see only one runner who was anywhere near as big and heavy as himself, a boy with a St. Croix Middle School vest. Before he could begin to feel self-conscious, however, Mr. Walker said, "There's something we have to do before you run. Close in tight and put your hands together here." The team formed a tight circle and put their hands on Mr. Walker's. "Now say with me: We're walkers and runners, and runners and walkers; all together — we're Walker's Runners." Derek led them in a wild whoop at the end, and they stood grinning at one another. Toby felt the same strange mix of belonging and pride he'd felt the day before when he first put on his shirt, but the feeling was stronger this time.

Mr. Walker was giving a few last words of advice when the St. Croix coach blew a whistle and called the runners to the starting line. The coach described where they would run and said there would be markers — people to show them the way — at every turn on the course. "Any questions?" The runners were jogging on the spot, stretching leg muscles, putting their arms above their heads and bending and stretching each way. Toby just stood, wondering whether he should do the same. Derek was squatting low on one leg, stretching the other leg out. The St. Croix coach concluded: "Remember, everybody, you're all winners, just by being here and taking part. We're proud of you whether you come first or last or anywhere in between, whether it takes five minutes or five hours to complete the course. Now, ready, set, *go!*"

Toby was swept forward in a surging crush of runners. Mr. Walker had told them, "Pace yourself. Don't worry about keeping up, especially at the beginning. Start slow and steady." But Toby couldn't get out of the jostling, racing pack and was running faster than he'd ever run before. The first part of the course took the runners around the perimeter of the field. The first marker was waving them on and pointing to the next section of the trail leading into the woods, which lay on two sides of the field. Toby's legs were shaking and his chest was heaving and pain was shooting up the side of his body but he could not slow down. The one time he tried to slow down, a lanky student ran into him from behind, knocking him to one side, where another student, a stocky girl on the Westfield Ridge team, scraped her sneaker down his shin as she tried to avoid him.

Before long, runners were passing him on both sides as the leaders drew ahead and the group began to thin and straggle. Soon he found himself on the edge of the pack of runners. Making sure no-one was close behind him, he slowed carefully to an unsteady shuffle. Daphne was just ahead of him, struggling almost as desperately. She gasped, "Do you want me to wait for you?" Toby waved her on, unable to find the breath to speak.

Looking ahead to where the course entered the trees, he saw Derek among the first runners, his arms pumping and his feet seeming to flash over the ground in long strides. Not far behind he saw Jason, Nicholas and Silas, and further back the twins. As he watched, the leaders disappeared into the trees, then the middle group, who were falling behind at every step, and finally the stragglers, Daphne among them, who turned to give him a little wave as she disappeared from his sight. The first marker was waving him forward and pointing him on to the woodland trail. Toby shuffled past. As he turned the first bend on the narrow, muddy trail, behind him he saw the marker jog away across the field, his job done. Toby was the last of the runners.

In the seclusion of the woods, with no-one behind, and the rest getting further and further ahead, he slowed his shuffle run to a walk. His side ached and his legs wobbled violently. He put his hand out to steady himself against a tree beside the trail. The tree rushed toward him and landed bruisingly against his shoulder. The ground seemed to be far away, as if he was seeing it through the wrong end of a telescope, then it, too, hurtled at him, smearing mud and dead leaves on his hands and knees as he tried to steady himself, animal like, on all fours. His eyes focussed in and out on the muddy imprints of running shoes. He tried to gasp in air, but his stomach heaved, and instead of air going in, vomit gushed out of his mouth and dribbled through his nose. The trees were whirling and spinning as he rolled on to his side on the lonely woodland trail.

* * *

That was where they found him, Mr. Walker and Derek coming in from the field, Daphne, the twins and Conrad through the woods.

Daphne said, "I knew he'd be around here somewhere. I could tell he wasn't feeling well."

Mr. Walker knelt in the mud beside Toby. "Can you stand?"

Toby had passed out for only a few seconds after throwing up, but when he'd opened his eyes he'd still felt dizzy. His shoulder was sore from falling against the tree, but he didn't think he was seriously hurt. However, the thought of getting to his feet, setting off through the woods and finishing the course had overwhelmed him. So even when the dizziness stopped, Toby had kept lying where he'd fallen. It wasn't the physical effort of finishing that had been so daunting, so much as the thought of emerging from the woods — supposing he got that far — and being confronted at the finish line by the runners who would have long finished, and by the parents and spectators and teachers. He imagined all of them watching the lone runner, muddy and bedraggled, with vomit on his vest, struggling home, in a distant last place. When he imagined it, his eyes had filled with tears. He had heard the familiar voices approaching from both sides. He had heard his name being called, but his shame and embarrassment were so great that he froze in self pity.

Now Conrad was on the other side of him from Mr. Walker, and he felt himself lifted from the ground, one arm around Conrad's shoulders, the other around Mr. Walker's. His feet stumbling between the adults, he was half carried and half dragged across the field to Conrad's truck. Derek, Daphne and the twins followed, grave faced, even the twins. Conrad and Mr. Walker helped him in. Toby hadn't spoken a word since they found him. He was glad that there were only a few runners and spectators still around.

The St. Croix coach jogged over and said, "Everything alright?" When Mr. Walker nodded, the coach said to Toby, "Tough luck. You were doing well. We're proud of you."

Toby hung his head and still said nothing. Daphne, Derek and the twins watched in a silent group.

Mr. Walker said, mockingly stern but kindly, "If you let this stop you running, I'll be mighty upset. The next meet is coming right up. There'll be no practices in between unless you want to take yourself for a run. I want to see you there."

Conrad nodded at Mr. Walker. He squeezed Toby's shoulder. Toby sat with his head down and said nothing.

11

Personal Worst

At recess the next day, Silas taunted: "Hey, Toby, what was wrong with you yesterday?" Toby ignored him, turning away and opening a box of raisins, his morning snack. Silas continued, "Did you see the fat kid from St. Croix, the one about the same size as you?"

Toby remembered seeing him before the race, and at the starting line-up, and he'd been briefly beside him in the crush of runners after the start. But after that he'd lost sight of him — and of all the other runners when they entered the woods.

Silas went on: "He finished in the first twenty. So what's wrong with you, that you couldn't even get half way round the course without collapsing?"

Toby carefully put his box of raisins in his pocket, and turning quickly, was about to grab Silas by the front of his shirt when Derek's voice stopped him.

"You guys, cut it out. What's going on, anyway?"

"Ask him," said Toby.

"Just talking about the meet," said Silas.

"I can imagine," said Derek. "I heard the bit about collapsing."

"It was just a bit of fun."

"You mean it was just to torment him. We're supposed to be a team, remember? Walker's Runners. We help each other; we don't torment each other. Now — shake hands, teammates."

Silas looked at Toby, and back at Derek.

"Do it," said Derek.

Silas slowly held out his hand toward Toby, who hesitated a moment, then grasped it. Silas' hand looked like a little kid's in Toby's large, muscular clasp.

"Teammates. Remember that," Derek said. "We've got another meet coming up."

Toby thought: I wonder if the big kid will be there. I'll watch him, because if he can finish well, then so can I. But how *does* he do it?

* * *

He was still pondering that question after recess, in French class, when Ms. Watkins broke into his reverie. "Toby. *Toby.* Are you listening? I said: what did we study in French yesterday?"

Toby said, "Don't you know?"

"Of course I know."

"Why are you asking me, then?"

Ms. Watkins sent him to the office, where Mr. Lowry said, glancing at the discipline report, "So you were rude to a teacher — again. How were you rude to Ms. Watkins? What did you say?"

Toby repeated the exchange he'd had with the French teacher.

"That's enough," said Mr. Lowry, holding up his hand like a policeman stopping traffic.

Toby went on, "I mean, I never could understand why teachers are always asking questions they already know the answer to ..."

"I said that's enough," Mr. Lowry said again.

"Like how many sides does an octagon have? Well if the teacher knows an octagon has eight sides, why is the teacher asking? And if the teacher doesn't know how many sides an octagon has, perhaps that teacher shouldn't be a teacher ..."

"*Toby Morton, be quiet!*" the principal thundered. "I'm tired of your rudeness, and I'm tired of your nonsense, and I'm tired of your wisecracks. It's time you got serious about something."

Mr. Lowry gave him detention for being rude, which gave Toby time to reflect: He really was getting serious about something. He was getting serious about his running, doing at least three practice runs a week, as well as skipping and dieting. And he was also getting serious about his whale project. He'd finished Why a Whale Is Not a Fish, and now he was working on The Parts of a Whale.

In class, when he started working on The Parts of a Whale he said to Mr. Walker, "I need to find a picture of a whale," and he overheard Nicholas snicker, "Try looking in a mirror."

Mr. Walker had snapped, "Teammates, remember, Nicholas?"

And Nicholas had mumbled, "Sorry."

* * *

At his next weigh-in with Amy, Toby asked about the big runner. "He's as — you know — as big as me, but he's a good runner. He must be, to finish in the first twenty out of all those runners. How does he do it?"

Amy said, "I guess he's just been practising longer. Come on. Let's go for a practice run now."

They walked and ran as far as Mrs. Evans' house and, turning around, stopped to rest.

"I could go a bit further," Toby said. He was amazed at how far he could go now. In an emergency, if he had to run to the telephone, he knew that at least he could get to Mrs. Evans' house, even if he still couldn't run all the way. "'Spose I'm getting fitter?"

"You must be, with the skipping and running and walking," said Amy. "And you're pacing yourself, too. That helps you go further because it saves your energy." Toby couldn't help grinning with pride. "You're finally getting serious about something," she added.

"Maybe you should tell that to Mr. Lowry," said Toby, thinking back to earlier that day.

Amy said, "When's the next meet?"

"Next Tuesday, at the school."

"That's so exciting. I wish I could come and watch, but Mum and me are going to the museum with the home schooling group that day. Are you excited, Toby, or are you worrying about it? Are you worrying, Toby?"

Toby confessed, "I'm worried about not finishing."

"But of course you'll finish. You know you can finish now."

"That's what I thought last time."

"But now you know about pacing yourself, and you've been running and skipping and walking lots since then. I just know you'll finish."

"Even if I finish, it'll be in last place."

"There's nothing wrong with being last. Someone's always got to be last."

"I don't just mean last. I mean last by a long way. I mean last coming in ages and ages after all the others have finished, and knowing people are laughing at you because you're so slow." He added cautiously, "I think perhaps I won't run."

Amy jumped up and put her hands on her hips.

Toby said, "Uh-oh."

"Now you listen to me, Toby Morton. We've been practising running, and we've been skipping and you've been dieting. Now don't you dare tell me you're going to give up now, just because you're afraid of coming in last. It doesn't matter where you come in and you know it. What matters is that you don't let your friends down — like Mr. Walker, and the other kids on the team. And me. You've just got to be more confident."

Toby said, "Yes, ma'am."

* * *

But confidence was the last thing on Toby's mind after school on Tuesday when he saw all the students who were staying to watch the race, and the buses pulling into the schoolyard bringing runners from the other schools, and parents and spectators arriving to watch the race. He was so nervous he was shaking and his teeth were chattering and he kept having to go to the bathroom. He'd been three times already since classes ended, and already he felt he wanted to go again. Despite Amy's encouragement, he still feared not being able to finish, and — even if he did finish — he feared coming in a humiliatingly distant last.

As the team gathered around Mr. Walker, Derek said, "Nervous, Toby?"

Toby could only nod.

"Me too," said Derek.

Mr. Walker reminded the team about aiming to do their personal best. "Winning isn't what matters most to cross-country runners. What matters most is doing a little bit better each time you race."

They performed the Walker's Runners chant and headed for the starting line. Toby muttered, "I've got to go to the bathroom," and slipped away, entering the school where he hid in the washroom, the same one he'd hidden in on the first day of term, afraid then of facing his new class. Now he was afraid of facing defeat and humiliation. Looking in the mirror, he told himself, *If you're going to be a failure, there's no point in making it worse by setting yourself up for even more humiliation, especially in front of kids who'll see you the next day, and who'll point at you, and say, There's the fat loser who thought he could run and who came in last by a couple of hours. It doesn't matter whether it's school work or cross-country running, it's best to play it safe, and to just not bother.*

Hearing cheers and applause, he peeked out of the bathroom window, but couldn't see the scene of the excitement. He ran through the school and went outside through the back door. He ran to the end of the building and peered cautiously around the corner as more cheers and applause erupted. Now he could see the runners setting off, his own team as well as the runners he remembered from the first meet. He saw the big runner from St. Croix. He saw Silas in the lead, with Derek and Jason and Nicholas, and the twins, also in the leading pack, and he felt a surge of pride and excitement. He saw Daphne already lagging behind, and willed her forward.

Suddenly, he found himself longing to be among them.

He started running toward the starting line, then checked himself before someone noticed. He'd said he was going to the bathroom; he couldn't suddenly appear on the playground. He'd have to emerge from the main door, where he'd entered. He turned back, ran around the school to the back door. He flew through the empty, echoing hallways to the main door, out of the school and across the yard. By the time he reached the starting line he was exhausted. He stood with his head bowed and his hands on his knees.

Mr. Walker called, "Okay, Toby?" But Toby was beyond speech and could only nod. Mr. Walker moved to him and said quietly, "I was afraid you weren't going to make it. Now, take your time. You don't have to run all the way."

"Run? I can't even walk."

"Remember you're aiming for *your* personal best."

"This is my personal best already. I wasn't going to run, you know. I was afraid. But at least I'm here. I guess that's going to be my personal best."

"No. Your personal best was getting half way round the course last time. This time — you finish."

"You hope."

"I *know*."

Toby gathered himself up. "Personal best? That's not what I'm about, is it, someone like me? How about personal worst? That'd be more like it. I'll aim for a personal worst instead of a personal best. Let me think. My personal worst is — okay — I will get back here."

Mr. Walker smiled. "Go for it, then. I'm proud of you. You know that."

Toby mimicked savagely, "'I'm proud of you.' For what? For running around and getting in a sweat? Big deal. Almost as big a deal as doing a stupid school project on whales." He looked at Mr. Walker to gauge the effect of his bitterness.

Mr. Walker smiled again, not rising to the bait. "Always the wisecracks. Go on. Get out of here. See you in a while."

Toby shuffled off in a half run, half walk, which he managed to sustain until he was behind the school and out of sight. He walked around the school, rested at the back for a few minutes, summoning some strength and breath, and then did his shuffle walk-run as he came briefly in sight again of the start, and of the spectators, before he left the school grounds and headed down Brunswick Street. He looked back once to make sure he was out of sight before stopping to rest again. Far ahead, he saw the leading pack, Derek and Silas among them, already at the end of the riverside trail, and heading across Main Street to the cemetery and to the Back Road. His feet seemed to be made of cement as he dragged himself slowly far behind them, from Brunswick Street onto the trail beside the river and across Main Street. He hadn't managed even a few steps of his shuffle walk-run since leaving the school grounds, and he'd completely forgotten Amy's advice to "walk a hundred, run a hundred." When he reached the cemetery he could barely walk. He sat on a gravestone to rest. He could just make out the faded inscription on the stone. It said: "A rest well earned."

This must have been put here for me, Toby muttered. He sat for a long time, gathering his strength and his will to continue.

From his seat, he could see through the trees to Main Street, where the afternoon traffic had thinned to just an occasional vehicle. He realised it must be getting late. He saw the twins pass in their minivan, their mother at the wheel. He wondered whether Daphne and the slower runners had finished, too, and whether he was the only one not finished. At last he heaved himself to his feet and set off again at a walk. Dusk was setting in as he left the cemetery and turned into the Back Road. Sauntering sadly along, he thought: *This is stupid. There's no point in finishing. Why don't I just quit now and head for home?* But something kept him plodding on, his hands thrust deep in the pockets of his new running shorts.

When he reached the Back Road mini-mall, he looked longingly into the window of the grocery store, at the bottles of pop and bags of chips on display. His mouth watered at the thought of them. He imagined the comfort he would feel strolling along the Back Road, a bag of chips in one hand, a bottle of pop in the other, stopping for a nibble and a gulp. But then he thought of Amy's disappointment at his next weigh-in if he didn't continue to lose weight, and he resisted the temptation.

He dragged himself slowly on, into the dark beyond the lights of the mini-mall, through the pool of light thrown by a gas station (they sold chips and pop in their little convenience store, too, he remembered), through the darkness where an arm of the cemetery ran down to the Back Road. All thought of running, even walking briskly, had long passed, and all Toby could do in his exhaustion was concentrate on placing one weary foot beyond the other. He wasn't even breathing heavily now. He gulped air in short gasps because it hurt his chest to take more in. His side ached with a dull persistence. His feet hurt and his legs threatened to collapse under him if they bent, so he kept them painfully locked straight.

He dragged himself past the lighted windows of Hatt's Autoparts and Accessories, stumbling on the gravel that had been thrown up by cars entering the parking lot beside the store. He leaned briefly against the window of Back Street Video, looking at the new video releases. He wondered why he seemed to care more about putting himself through this running torture than about settling down after school with a video and a bag of chips like he used to. Beyond the lights of the video store, and beyond a patch of scrubby, alder-strewn ground, he could see the school's back field, and the back entrance to the field halfway along it. He hoped there was no-one left at school to witness his shame and embarrassment at coming in so late — not just last, but *way* last, so far last that it was going to be nearly completely dark before he reached the finishing line.

He crossed the field, feeling the evening damp rising through his shoes and curling around his legs. He stumbled and nearly fell as his new running sneakers moved from the grass of the field to the gravel of the playground. He drove his legs the last few steps around the school. There was no sign of anyone, runners or spectators.

He thought: Good. That will spare me some of my shame. At least until the teasing starts tomorrow. But teasing was nothing new to him. The only new thing was the fact that he was giving kids something extra to tease him about: his running.

In spite of his relief at there being no-one around, he felt a nagging disappointment. Was that how little Mr. Walker cared, so little that he couldn't even wait for Toby to get back? Even after saying, "I'm proud of you. See you in a while"? So what if it was a long time to wait. He might at least have been there to see Toby finish.

The finishing line had been two red pylons near the main door, and like the runners and the spectators, the pylons were no longer there. Toby saw this with a final pang of humiliation and disappointment. Mr. Walker cared so little for his completing the course that he hadn't bothered to wait for him to come in, and he'd even cleared away the finishing line.

After all his effort, Toby couldn't even cross the finishing line, because it wasn't there.

He turned toward the door. He'd change and go home. Now he knew just how stupid he'd been, and how stupid he looked, to have driven himself so hard and so desperately to finish a stupid cross-country running race.

No runners. No spectators. No finishing line. No coach.

No care!

He spoke his bitterest thought aloud: "And I'll put this running gear where I should have put it in the first place. In the garbage."

A voice came out of the dark. "It's over here, Toby."

Mr. Walker emerged from the shadows near the school, carrying the two red pylons.

"What's over there?"

"The finishing line. I thought you were looking for it."

"I was looking for signs of human existence."

"Am I human enough?"

"I guess so — for a teacher."

"Thanks. I'm glad you can still make your wisecracks. Come and cross the line. I had to move it to let some cars out. But here you are now."

Mr. Walker placed the pylons in position. Toby hesitated, took two defiant steps toward the school, then stopped. He turned, and advanced painfully and slowly towards the pylons.

He stopped at the line and said bitterly, "I now pronounce this not just my personal worst, but the worst of anybody, anywhere, in the history of cross-country running."

He stepped forward. Solitary clapping came from the shadows, and Derek stepped forward. Mr. Walker clapped, too.

Toby hung his head. "Yeah. Huge applause for the biggest failure in the world. Thank you. Thank you. Thank you."

Mr. Walker said, "But Toby, you made it."

"All I made was a fool of myself."

12

Disgrace

After collapsing at the first meet, nearly failing to start at the second meet, and then coming in so long after all the other runners, Toby thought he could endure no greater shame and humiliation in his brief cross-country running career. But after the third meet, he knew that he was wrong. It could get worse. There was a greater shame and humiliation.

There was disgrace.

The meet was at Keswick Narrows, a few kilometres upriver from Brunswick Valley. His mother drove him there after school. Conrad was going to take him but had to work, and Mrs. Morton said, "I don't know why you want to waste your time with this running, but I suppose I might as well come and see what you're up to."

As they drove into the town, Toby gazed at the houses, which seemed bigger and newer and more spaced out than the ones in Brunswick Valley. It was like one big, smart subdivision. The school itself, Keswick Narrows Memorial, was new. It had landscaped grounds more like a park than a schoolyard, with trees and flower beds and benches. The school consisted of six low, white buildings and a higher central building connected by glass walkways. Toby thought Keswick Narrows Memorial looked like a space station.

The team gathered around Mr. Walker just before the start as he reminded them, "Pace yourselves. Don't get in a panic if you feel yourself lagging behind at the start. Save your energy, and when you feel you've got some to spare, then you can increase your pace. But if you can't — it doesn't matter! Remember it's your personal best you're aiming for. You all know what that is, because we've talked about it. Derek, if you're aiming for the provincial team, you need a top three finish, inside twenty minutes again. Jason, Nicholas and Silas, you'll help pace Derek through the early stages and your goal is to place in the top twenty. Twins — top twenty as well. Daphne, you're aiming to get round the course inside thirty-five minutes. Toby, your personal best will be to finish inside three quarters of an hour."

Toby grumbled, "It's the worst personal best of the team. All I'm good for is personal worst."

"Cut it out, Toby. Stop feeling sorry for yourself," Mr. Walker admonished sternly. "Now, everyone ready?"

They all nodded. Toby wondered whether he should go to the bathroom again, but told himself it was just nerves making him think he wanted to go. He was shaking and his teeth were chattering with nervousness again. He forced the images of the first and second meets from his mind, of his lonely collapse in the woods at St. Croix, of his late finish in the dusk at Brunswick Valley, and tried to focus on the run at hand. Derek, sensing his unease, gave him a thumbs-up and Mr. Walker winked. Daphne maneuvered herself beside him and looked at him from the corners of her eyes. When a member of the Westfield Ridge team passed by and laughed, "Hey, the Brunswick Valley tub's here again," Silas told him to shut up.

"One more thing before you start," said Mr. Walker. "Ready?" They huddled in a group. "We're runners and walkers, walkers and runners; all together — we're Walker's Runners." Their hands shot skywards from the middle of their circle and they whooped in unison. Toby felt again that strange wonderful feeling of belonging, of people helping one another, and helping him. The feeling seemed to get stronger at every meet, despite the setbacks.

He was feeling good, despite his nervousness. At his last weigh-in with Amy and her mother he found he'd lost another five pounds, and he fancied he could even see himself looking better. "I'm a little bit trimmer, I think," was how he'd put it, hesitantly, to Amy and her mother, and they agreed.

As the teams moved toward the starting line he saw the big runner from St. Croix and wondered again how he managed to run so well. He wondered, too, if he dared ask him. He saw his mother waving to him from the crowd of parents and spectators at the starting line. She was wearing a yellow pant suit and a straw hat with flowers stuck in the brim. Embarrassed, Toby pretended not to notice, until Daphne said, "Toby, isn't that your mom, waving?" and then he had to give a little wave. Daphne said wistfully, "You're lucky, having your mom come and watch you."

Toby turned to her to ask why her mom hadn't come, realising he knew nothing about Daphne's life outside school. But before he could ask, the Keswick Narrows coach started to describe the course. It would take them through the landscaped grounds of the school to the road, which they were to follow as far as the municipal park. There they were to follow the nature trail which went in a big loop through the wooded area of the park, and finally they would rejoin the road for the return journey.

"Everybody understand? Any questions? In that case — ready, set, *go!*"

As the jostling crowd of runners surged forward in a mass of swirling elbows and kicking legs, Toby repeated to himself, *Pace yourself. Pace yourself. Let the leaders go. Let them go. Don't worry about falling back.*

That was happening already, but he had enough experience now not to get drawn into an attempt to keep up with the leaders. He recalled his aim: To finish inside three quarters of an hour, and that was plenty of time, he told himself. He'd added a second personal-best goal, without telling anyone: To finish not too far behind all the others, and if he wasn't absolutely last, that would be a bonus.

He saw Derek and the other boys in the leading pack, as usual. They were in a tight group, Silas leading, with Derek hard on his heels, almost treading on them, followed by Nicholas and Jason. As Toby watched, Silas dropped back and Nicholas moved up to take his place. That must be what they mean by pacing Derek in the early stages, he thought. At the same time as he felt an astonishing, daunting gulf between their running ability and his, he felt proud of himself to be at least taking part in a race with them, and he felt proud of them, and of all his teammates. He could see the twins not too far behind the leaders, and even from his place near the back he could still hear them laughing. He envied them their high spirits.

Daphne was running beside him. As they turned from the road into the municipal park, they passed the first marker, and Daphne said, "I'm going to move up a bit. Is that okay?"

Toby waved her on, feeling his legs weakening and his lungs starting to hurt. He was falling further and further behind all the other runners, and was telling himself not to worry about it. He still managed to keep up his shuffle run, which was turning into his shuffle walk-run as he passed the next marker, who pointed him on to the nature trail. Suddenly, he was alone on the trail. He stopped and rested his hands on his knees, feeling dizzy and sick.

Not again, he thought, and looked up to try and focus on something distant to stop the dizziness. He searched for a tree, or a bush, or a stump to fix his eyes on. Instead he saw the heavy runner from St. Croix; saw him look quickly and carefully around, missing Toby because he was still stooped so low. Toby saw his counterpart suddenly leave the trail and plunge into the trees. It took him a few moments to realise what the St. Croix runner was up to.

He thought: The nature trail goes in a big loop through the woods. If you cut across the loop, it'd be a short cut. It'd bring you out at the other end of the nature trail, just before it rejoins the road.

While the other runners ran all the way round, you'd cruise through the short cut and come out just ahead of them, or just behind them.

They'd be sweaty and tired. You'd be cool and refreshed.

They'd struggle to keep running to the finish. You'd have lots of energy to keep up with them — or even to overtake them — and finish in a respectable place.

Brilliant!

Toby straightened up and hurried to the place where he'd seen the St. Croix runner leave the trail. He paused and looked around. No-one was in sight. All the runners were far ahead, and there were no more markers until the trail came out at the road. He stepped off the trail into the woods. He stopped.

He thought of Mr. Walker. How would he feel if he could see Toby now, about to take a short cut?

Cheating.

How would Derek feel?

How would Daphne and the twins feel? What would Silas and Nicholas and Jason say if they knew he cheated? Wouldn't that make him an even bigger loser in their eyes?

Maybe they'd be right.

And what would Amy say? Had she helped him with all the running and healthy eating just so that he could cheat?

Toby couldn't do it. He turned back onto the trail and plodded forward, resigned to being, yet again, a distant last place finisher.

Then he stopped again.

The more he thought about the short cut, and the St. Croix runner using it even now, the angrier he got. He thought of how adults like Mr. Walker and Amy's mum and Conrad kept saying things like, "We're proud of you."

Proud? Of cheating?

But even as Toby's anger grew, it was replaced by a different feeling. First he felt guilt at his anger — because wasn't he thinking of doing just the same thing? Then he felt sympathy for the cheating runner. Why was he cheating? Could it be because he, too, was teased about his size? While Toby had been driven to wisecracking and eating by the endless teasing, had the St. Croix runner been driven to cheating as the only way he could gain some pride in himself?

Propelled forward by the unexpected sympathy he felt, Toby plunged through the grabbing alders and tripping bracken until, with a desperate burst of speed, he caught up with the cheating runner. He grabbed him by the shoulder and swung him round.

"Where do you think you're going?"

"Where do you think, stupid?"

"Cheating's stupid."

"No. Getting caught is stupid, stupid."

"You're wrong. Just finishing is good enough."

"Good enough for you, maybe."

"I'm getting better. I won't always be last."

"You really think so, carrying all that blubber around with you? Get real, fat boy. The only reason you're here is because you think you're going to get some kind of respect from all those jocks who laugh at you, right?"

Toby hung his head, recognising the truth.

"Right?" the runner said again.

Toby said nothing.

The St. Croix runner went on, "Well I've got news for you. You're still a loser. You're still a fat loser. And all fat losers get is laughed at. Well I may be fat, but I'm not going to be a loser, and I don't care how. So get out of my way, blubber boy."

Toby reeled in dismay. He'd expected the St. Croix runner to share his feelings of sympathy. Instead, he'd been received with anger and contempt. The shock of it was all the more painful because the contempt and insults came from someone who suffered like him.

The runner pushed Toby backward into the brush and set off again through the trees. Toby scrambled up and lunged after him. He almost had hold of his shirt when a voice said, "You two. What do you think you're doing?"

Toby hadn't noticed how close they were to the trail, and he hadn't noticed the course marker positioned to point the way from the nature trail to the road leading back to the finishing line.

"Nice going, stupid," said the St. Croix runner viciously.

"Sorry," Toby said. Then, when the marker ordered, "You two, wait here," Toby again said, "Sorry." He wasn't sure why he said it, or who he was saying it to.

The marker said to Toby, "I know that cheating isn't something you learned from Mr. Walker."

The last group of runners appeared and the marker pointed them toward the road, saying, "Go, runners. You're only five minutes from home!" Daphne was among them, and gave Toby a curious, puzzled look as she passed. Then the marker led the boys onto the road and they set off, walking toward Keswick Narrows Memorial school. In the distance, Toby saw the stragglers enter the school grounds, and guessed when they crossed the finishing line from the applause and encouraging cries he heard coming from the spectators.

Fleetingly, longingly, Toby wondered what it would feel like to be the proud centre of those cries and that applause.

Then the marker said, "You two, let's see what your coaches have to say about cheating." He marched them in ignominious disgrace toward the finishing line under the silent, wondering gaze of the other runners and spectators.

13

Toby's Resolution

They followed the marker toward the finishing line. When Toby saw they were heading straight for it, he carefully made a detour to avoid crossing it. The St. Croix runner didn't seem to notice the finishing line at all and just kept going.

The Keswick Narrows coach asked, "What have we got here?"

"A couple of runners who thought they'd take a short cut through the woods," the marker said, and went on to explain how he'd encountered the boys emerging from the trees.

Mr. Walker and the St. Croix coach each left their teams, which had gathered around them for congratulations, and walked over to where Toby and his co-accused waited.

The Keswick Narrows coach said, "I'm afraid it looks as if temptation got the better of these two. They were caught taking a short cut."

The St. Croix coach said, "Is that right?" and then to his runner, "I guess this will be your last race. I'm not tolerating cheating."

"Who wants your stupid cross-country races anyway?" the St. Croix runner said.

Mr. Walker looked at Toby and raised his eyebrows. "We'll talk about this tomorrow, Toby."

The runners from the different schools were standing in a hushed group, sensing that something serious was going on, wondering what it was. Toby, with his head down, walked through them to where his mother waited in the truck.

As they drove home Mrs. Morton asked, "Was it a good race, then, lovey?" Toby said nothing. "I liked watching you all set off. That was the most exciting part, that and seeing you come back again. I thought you'd be left far behind, but there you were, still just about keeping up with the others at the finish. Wasn't it nice of that man to walk the last bit of the race with you? When's your next race, anyway? I wouldn't mind coming to watch you again."

Toby said nothing.

When they reached home, Conrad was stacking wood in the yard. Toby heard him call, "How'd it go, big guy?" but he ignored him. He ran out of the yard and set off up the hill, still in his running gear. He'd never run all the way up the hill before, even when he and Amy did their practice runs, but this time he reached the top with ease and sped off on their usual practice route. He wondered, as his feet pounded him along, where did this furious energy come from? Why couldn't he summon it at will, when he was running in a cross-country race, and not have to bring up the rear? He ran until he was exhausted, then jumped the roadside ditch and threw himself down at the edge of a blueberry field.

The fall leaves of the blueberries glowed a vivid red in the late evening sun. On the edge of the woods beyond the field two deer grazed. They sensed Toby's presence, even from across the field, and ran into the woods with astonishing, springing lightness, grace and speed. Toby wondered if they somehow knew hunting season would start soon, and were extra skittish because of it. He envied them their light swiftness. If he had that easy speed, he would have been with the front runners instead of the last, and would never have been tempted to cheat ...

He cut himself off abruptly. Now he was even doubting himself. He wasn't cheating. He was trying to prevent a fellow runner from cheating, not because he was jealous of the other's advantage, but because he wanted to help. And all he'd got for his trouble, and for his sympathy for another overweight runner (*there — you might as well say it,* he told himself — *another fat runner*), was bitter insults from the person he was trying to help and accusations of cheating from the adults.

He'd show them all. He'd … he'd … he'd give up running. He nodded his head firmly. That's what he'd do, to teach them all a lesson. He'd give up running.

"Toby?"

Amy's voice cut through his angry reverie.

"Toby?"

What would Amy say if he gave up running? He'd miss their runs.

"Where are you, Toby?"

What would Derek and Daphne and the twins say if he gave up running? He'd miss their camaraderie and friendship.

"Toby, I know you're 'round here somewhere."

What would Mr. Walker say? He'd miss his insistence that Toby succeed.

"There you are. I knew you were here somewhere. I saw you run up the hill and I guessed that something was wrong. Something *is* wrong, isn't it, Toby? What is it? What happened? Did something happen at the meet? Did it, Toby?"

Amy sat beside him. He turned to her. She was blurry. He blinked, but she turned blurry again. He hadn't realised he was crying. He turned away, embarrassed.

"Was it something bad, Toby? Did you collapse? Did you come in late, Toby? That doesn't matter. Just doing your best is what—"

"They said I cheated," he interrupted.

Amy stopped, cut off in mid-sentence, her mouth open. Toby looked at the distant woods. They were even blurrier.

"Oh, Toby."

"I didn't."

"I know you didn't, Toby."

"They said I did."

"Who said?"

"The marker, and the coaches."

"Mr. Walker said you cheated?"

"Well, no, not Mr. Walker. He said we'd talk about it tomorrow."

"Oh, Toby. What happened?"

Toby shook his head. Blinked away tears, bringing the world back into focus. The deer were back, grazing on the far side of the field, oblivious to, or grown familiar with, Toby and his small troubles. He told Amy how he'd felt almost confident at the start of the race. How he'd remembered to pace himself. How he hadn't worried too much when he started to fall behind. And then, the fleeting moment of temptation, to cheat, and how it was replaced by sympathy for a runner like him, struggling with weight and teasing.

"I mean, he was as ... as ... as big as me." Amy nodded. "And that's why he was taking the short cut, because he was ... overweight ... and he'd been teased about it. I know that's why he did it. It was his way of getting back at the kids who called him names." Amy nodded again. "Then he called me names. He called me ... he called me ... fat boy, and blubber boy. And I was trying to help."

Fury was mounting in Toby again, drumming blood in his ears, speeding his pulse, reddening his face.

Amy put her hand on his arm. "You're really upset and mad, aren't you, Toby? And you really want to show them, don't you?" He nodded, drawing a shuddering, shaky breath.

A bank of heavy, grey evening clouds had moved across the sky as the friends talked. Just as the sun was about to drop below the horizon, the clouds parted, and a slant of sunlight turned the woods golden-green, the blueberry field a fiery red. The deer, disturbed by something unseen and unheard by the friends — a hunter, scouting the woods, perhaps, Toby thought — skittered back into the trees.

Toby nodded to himself. He knew the best way to show them.

* * *

In the morning, despite his resolution, he skulked through the hallway to class with his head down. Of his teammates he'd seen only the twins, whose smiles faded when they saw him, whether from sympathy or contempt Toby didn't know. Bleakly he wondered whether they'd ever stopped smiling before. He arrived at the classroom door. Silas, Jason and Nicholas were already at their desks and looked up at him. As he braced himself for their rubbing of salt into the wound of his humiliation, Mr. Lowry's voice snapped behind him.

"Toby Morton. My office. Now."

Mr. Walker came, too, although the principal hadn't asked him.

As soon as they were in the principal's office, Mr. Lowry announced, "I want him off the team. No. I don't just want him off the team. I want him *out of this school.*"

Mr. Walker countered resolutely, "That's absurd."

"Don't tell me what's absurd. I have the responsibility of running this school and that includes taking all the steps necessary for maintaining discipline and decorum. And if that boy thinks he can not only get away with doing hardly a stroke of work, but also with being rude to his teachers, and now with cheating when representing the school, then he'd better think again."

"You're over-reacting. Toby wasn't—"

"Over-reacting? When it's a blatant, shameless example of cheating?"

"It was a misunderstanding. And Toby is making progress at school. He's been working harder, he's trying to keep his wisecracks appropriate, and he's got himself involved in some healthy physical exercise for the first time. I'm telling you, he's making progress, and I don't want to see that progress spoiled by hasty over-reaction to a thoughtless, spur-of-the-moment mistake."

It was like watching a game of tennis. Toby's head moved from side to side as he followed the speeches of the principal and Mr. Walker. And he was the ball, being slammed by the principal and defended by Mr. Walker.

A fierce drive from the principal: "He's graduated from laziness to cheating. Is that what you call progress?"

A weak lob from Mr. Walker: "It wasn't so much cheating as ..."

A smash from the principal: "The school has zero tolerance for cheating in sports. You know that. I'm suspending him from school."

A desperate retrieval from Mr. Walker: "Suspension? What good will that do? He'll—"

A brutal, clinching volley from the principal, cutting off Mr. Walker in mid-stroke: "I'm no longer interested in what's good for him. I'm concerned with what's good for the school."

But Mr. Walker wasn't finished yet. Not only did he retrieve again, gallantly and desperately, but he managed to turn his retrieval into an attack: "May I suggest that it's what's good for your reputation that you should be interested in, especially with the school review coming up?"

Mr. Lowry faltered: "What do you mean?"

"I'm sure the review committee will be interested to read in my comments on the principal that he puts the well-being of his students above everything else."

The principal, mollified, managed only a weak shot in return: "Well, if you put it like that ..."

Mr. Walker followed up brilliantly: "If Toby achieves success, of any kind, academic or sporting, it will be a tribute to your concern for him, and to your good judgement in dealing with him."

Game, set and match to Mr. Walker. Toby wanted to applaud.

* * *

After the heated, tennis-like argument between Mr. Walker and Mr. Lowry, Mr. Walker said, "Toby, come with me. Tell me what happened."

They sat in a corner of the library.

"I thought you knew what happened. You just told Mr. Lowry it was a misunderstanding. Then you said it was a thoughtless, spur-of-the-moment mistake. That's what you said."

"I know what I said. I still need to know what happened."

"I wasn't cheating."

"I know that, too."

"How do you know, if you don't know what happened?"

"I just know you wouldn't do that."

There was a pause, then Toby said, "I guess I should say thank you, for stopping Mr. Lowry from suspending me."

"You don't have to say thank you. But you do have to tell me what happened, so that I can explain it to the team."

"Just tell them I wasn't cheating."

"I've told them that already. But I still need to know what happened, so that I can explain it to them, and to the principal. You better know that the St. Croix student is off the team —

his coach told me last night — and that means Mr. Lowry's going to be under pressure to do the same."

"It would be easier if you just put me off the team, wouldn't it?"

"I'm not interested in what's easier. I'm interested in the truth."

"Do *you* want me off the team?"

Mr. Walker sighed, exasperated. "No. I've told you. I believe you — so of course I don't want you off the team."

"Do the others? Derek and the rest?"

"No — especially when I tell them what happened."

Toby watched Miss Little's kindergarten students arrive at the library door in their silent line. They stopped and waited for permission to enter, as Mr. Walker went on, "So stop putting yourself down and looking for your own easy way out — because that's what being forced to quit would be — and tell me what happened at the meet yesterday."

Toby told the whole story, of being tempted to take the short cut, then wanting to stop the St. Croix runner, because he understood why he was cheating and wanted to help. When he finished, he shrugged and said, "I was pretty stupid, huh?"

Mr. Walker shook his head. "No. You were pretty brave, I think. I'm proud of you."

"How come you believe me?"

Mr. Walker said gently, "Because I trust you."

Toby thought for a moment, shrugged again, and said, "But you believed me right off. Before I even explained what really happened, you believed me when I said I wasn't cheating. Why?"

Mr. Walker said again, "Because I trust you."

Miss Little walked forward from the end of the line of her waiting students and, seeing Mr. Walker and Toby in conversation in the library, held up a hand for her class to wait. Mr. Walker beckoned her in, then leaned forward and went on:

"Now, Toby, I've told you what I want you to do. But you have to decide what *you* want to do, because you know some of the runners on the other teams are still going to be suspicious. Can you handle that?"

"I think so."

Miss Little, passing the table with her perfectly behaved students, smiled and winked at Toby.

He straightened up. "Yes, I can handle it. I want to show them something. I decided last night. I want to show them I *can* run."

14

Running Feet

Mr. Walker had often talked to the team about feeling a rhythm in their steps when they were running, and about letting that rhythm drive them forward. Toby had never understood what he meant — until now.

It was Saturday morning, two weeks after the shameful meet, and he and Amy had passed Mrs. Evans' house, then turned off the road to town onto a dirt road. They were two kilometres from their homes on the hill, running between the meadows on St. David's Ridge, where the woods gave way to a long-abandoned farm. This was now the friends' turning around place. Toby wheeled in the road, turned back and resumed the rhythm he'd discovered that morning on the run out. He even had a rhyme going through his head, keeping time and driving the rhythm in his legs and feet:

"Running feet.
Take the heat.
Won't be beat,
At the meet."

The rhyme didn't make sense — but then neither did cross-country running, when you thought about it, except that it was fun, like the rhyme, which had just popped into his head as he ran. He felt as if he could run all day. At the weigh-in that morning with Amy and her mother, they found he'd lost another five pounds. Amy's mother had hugged him and said, "You're getting to be positively svelte."

"Positively what?" said Toby.

"Positively svelte."

"Sounds like a Swedish dress designer," said Toby.

But it was true, he was, well, not svelte (he'd looked it up — "slender or graceful in figure or outline" — and he definitely was not svelte, not yet, anyway), but he certainly wasn't as fat. And he felt svelte! His mother had even talked of taking him into town to the Second Time Around store, to get him some clothes, and when he'd been helping Conrad stack wood the night before, he'd caught Conrad watching him.

"What's up?" Toby asked.

"Nothing, except ... you're looking good, you know, big guy. Good for you."

Now he could see Amy ahead of him — way ahead, as usual — but he knew he'd make it to where she was now, and after that he'd make it to the "finishing line" at their houses on the hill. He knew he wouldn't collapse, or make a fool of himself in some way, like he had at the meets. He pushed away those bitter memories, and replaced them with the thought that he could easily run for help if Amy should ever have another asthma attack.

She was running on the spot, letting him catch up. When he came alongside her, she said, "Let's rest."

"I don't need to."

"I know — but I do."

They sat on a rock at the edge of the meadows, their legs sticking out into the dusty road.

Amy said, "So you're back in Keswick Narrows next week for the last meet of the season. That's so exciting. Can Mum and I come and watch?"

"I suppose so — if you really want to, and if you've really got nothing better to do. Ma and Con are taking me over. You could get a ride with them."

"But I don't want to come if you're going to ... you know ..."

"Collapse? Arrive back after dark? Look as if I'm taking a short cut? Don't worry. I won't embarrass you."

"I didn't mean that, Toby. You know I didn't mean that. I wouldn't be embarrassed if any of those things happened. It's just that ... I wouldn't know what to do, Toby. I don't think I could bear to see you so ... so sad and forlorn again, like you were after the last meet."

"Don't worry," Toby said again. "Mr. Walker and I have set two goals for this time. Well, he set one and I've set one. His is — I'm going to finish inside thirty-five minutes, and mine is — I'm not going to be last! That'll be my personal best." Toby added, "It's a pretty pathetic 'personal best,' but it's the best I can come up with."

* * *

The day of meet number four was also the day when Toby was to present his whale project to the class. He stood sheepishly at the front of the room and started, "How many of you have seen a whale?"

Most hands went up, and one of the boys said, "I'm looking at one right now."

Jason, Nicholas, Silas and Daphne said at the same time, "Shut up, you," and Mr. Walker threatened the boy, "One more comment like that and you'll be in detention. Go on, please, Toby."

Toby continued: "Well, my mammal project is on whales, because I like them. The more I find out about them, the more I like them. First I'm going to tell you," he looked down at his project, "Why a Whale is Not a Fish."

By the time Toby reached his last section, "My Favourite Whale," he was so absorbed in sharing his project that he'd almost forgotten to be self-conscious. "There are about seventy-five types of whales, and my favourite is the right whale. It's called the 'right' whale because it was the 'right' one to hunt. It got hunted because it has a thick body covered in blubber and, although it's powerful, it's slow. This made it an easy target, and it was hunted, mercilessly and cruelly.

"I found this poem."

Toby held up his drawing of a right whale as he recited from memory:

The right whale
Was the "right" whale
To hunt and to kill.
If the right whale
Was the wrong whale
There'd be lots of them still.

He didn't let on that he'd made up the poem himself.

15

Not Last

There was a crush of spectators and runners at Keswick Narrows Memorial School.

"Walker's Runners — here, please." Mr. Walker's voice rose above the excited clamour. "Everyone ready — for the last meet of the year? First, I want you all to know how proud I am of how you've run this season. You've been more than just a good bunch of runners. You've become a good team, looking out for each other and helping each other — and not just in races. And that's what a team is all about." They all looked at one another, smiling and a little embarrassed by Mr. Walker's praise.

Their coach went on: "Now, you've all got your personal bests to aim for today. Derek, you're aiming to finish in the top three again, to make it top three every race this year, and your time's going to be within twenty minutes again. That means you're going to make the provincial team!"

They all applauded and cheered, while Derek protested, "It's thanks to you guys, especially Silas and Jason and Nicholas, pacing me and always driving me on. And don't forget I'll need that again today."

Mr. Walker continued, "Silas, twenty-two minutes and top six. Jason, Nicholas, twenty-five minutes and top ten, again. Twins, twenty-six minutes — and no stopping to laugh at anything on the way." Everyone laughed, the twins most of all. "Daphne, thirty minutes. Daphne?"

Daphne's head was hanging down. "I don't think I can do it."

"You can do it. You will do it. Right?" Everyone cheered again when Daphne looked up, bit her lip, and nodded. "And Toby, your personal best is to finish inside thirty-five minutes."

Toby nodded and Daphne smiled at him. Derek said, "Alright," and Silas slapped him on the back. Mr. Walker added dryly, slyly, "And you're going to stick to the trail." The team laughed and cheered again, as convinced as Toby of his innocence of any cheating.

Toby thought to himself: *Then there's my other personal best, which is that I'm not going to be last.*

He'd suggested this to Mr. Walker the day before, but Mr. Walker had said stick to a time goal. "I don't want you getting disappointed," he'd added, gently.

But Toby was sure that now he was ready not just to run, but to be a competitor. The idea had come to him after he'd presented his whale project to the class.

* * *

There had been a long pause after he finished his presentation, then Mr. Walker had said, "Thank you, Toby. That's an impressive piece of work. You gave us lots of information, and you presented it well. I'm giving your project an 'A'."

Toby was so surprised that he hadn't even come up with a wisecrack in response. He couldn't remember when he'd last had an 'A.' He couldn't remember if he'd ever had an 'A.' Certainly he couldn't remember when he'd last cared whether or not he had an 'A' — or an 'F.' As he'd returned to his seat, he'd noticed Daphne looking at him. He couldn't decide quite how she was looking at him, but he thought she looked — well —

proud of him. And Jason and Nicholas and Silas had looked not just stunned, but admiring, too, and not grudgingly so.

As he sat down, Toby had a sudden insight: *I can do this school stuff! I'll never be as good as Daphne, but I can do it okay. And I'll never run as well as Derek the Red. Or even as well as the twins (although I might get to keep up with Daphne). But I'm an okay runner — and that's okay. I can do it. I'll never be a winner, but I don't* have *to be last.*

It was all to do with ... with ... confidence, in his running, and in himself.

He didn't have to be Toby the worst runner, or Toby the overweight runner, or Toby the best runner (he knew he'd never be that), but it was all right to be, just, Toby, the runner, and to be happy with that. And he didn't have to be Toby the wisecracking class clown, or Toby who never did his school work, but it was all right to be, just, Toby, the student, and to be happy with that.

Yes — he was happy, and proud, to be ... Toby.

* * *

He turned his attention back to Mr. Walker, who was saying, "For the last time this season, ready, everybody?"

They closed into a tight circle, hands joined in the centre, and chanted: "We're runners and walkers, walkers and runners; all together — we're Walker's Runners." Their hands soared up and they cheered in unison. The feeling of belonging was stronger than ever, too strong to be expressed, impossible to express anyway in the urgent, surging excitement.

The Keswick Narrows coach called the runners to the starting line and reminded them of the course they were to take, the same route as before. Toby could see his mother and Conrad, and Amy and her mother beside them, in the crowd that had gathered each side of the starting line. Looking at it, he reflected that as soon as the race had started this would become the finishing line, too. How good it must feel to cross that line, and to hear the applause and get congratulations, he thought.

"For the last time this season: Ready, set, *go!*"

A huge cheer. A surge of runners. Beware of elbows and feet. A glimpse of Amy and her mother, and his mother and Conrad, waving and smiling. And of Mr. Walker, brimming with excitement and enthusiasm, urging them on, and — oh! — Miss Little, too, beside him. Crowds thinning. Don't get caught up in the early rush to the front. Suddenly, no spectators around, just runners. The jostling bunch thinning. Stringing out.

Pace yourself.

Derek was in third place, already settling into the rhythmic swing of arms and legs that Toby envied, now that he was just beginning to understand it and feel it himself. Silas, Jason and Nicholas were separated from Toby by only a few runners, the twins, too. He could hear the twins laughing even as they ran. Daphne was in her usual early place beside him. They were in the middle of the second pack. Would this be the time he not only finished, but finished respectably placed?

But even as these thoughts crowded his head, and they passed the first marker, and even as he felt himself settling into his own recently discovered rhythm …

"Running feet.
Take the heat.
Won't be beat,
At the meet,"

… he realised, sadly, he was already falling back. Even Daphne, with a little, apologetic smile and wave, was leaving him behind.

Ahead, he saw the front running pack forming and moving away from the rest. Silas had moved up into second place, with Derek at his heels, so close that he was practically treading on them. Jason and Nicholas were tucked in close behind him, carrying out their team plan of pacing Derek and driving him to reach his best. Toby was proud to watch them, even as he fell further behind.

Well — remember — personal best. He knew he'd accomplish one of his aims: He knew he'd finish within his thirty-five minutes. As for the other, secret, personal best, of not finishing last, he saw it slipping away. He was already last, and lagging badly as he passed the second marker, who recognised him from previous meets. "This way. Take the trail into the woods. Keep going. You're going to make it," the marker called out as Toby chugged past, "You're going to make it. We're proud of you," he repeated. Toby looked back, smiled and managed a weak wave. The marker grinned and gave him the thumbs up.

He was slowing to a sad shuffle through the woods trail, nearing the place where he'd stopped, exhausted, on the previous run, and where he'd seen the St. Croix competitor setting off on the short cut, when Amy suddenly appeared beside him, running.

"Where did you come from?"

"I got Mum to drive me up the road and drop me off. She's waiting. I guessed that you'd be getting tired somewhere around here. But guess what, Toby. Just guess what!"

Toby rolled his eyes. "What?"

"I've got something to make you incredibly *un*tired."

"I hope you're not offering me performance enhancing drugs."

"'Course not, silly. It's not a drug. It's a new *system*. Another incredibly momentous system. It's so incredibly momentous it has to have capitals. It's a New System."

"That's just what I need. A New System."

"It came to me last night, all of a sudden, after you said you were aiming not to be last. It's wondrously brilliant. Come on, Toby. You're getting further behind. I'll explain as we run." She set off running, still talking, and Toby obediently followed. "You know that run-a-hundred, walk-a-hundred system? Well, that's a good system — but this is an even better system. It's so much better — that's fifty by the way — it's positively mind-bogglingly dazzlingly brilliant. Seventy-five." Toby, reduced now to his shuffle run, wondered fleetingly how Amy could not only run so lightly and effortlessly, but also talk and count at the same time. "One hundred ten."

He gasped. "Wait. One hundred ten. Now we walk."

Amy turned to him and said, running backwards, "No. That's the point, Toby. That's the *whole* point. We run *two* hundred. And that's one hundred fifty."

Toby was so aghast at the prospect of running two hundred steps that he was still running when Amy said, "Whoa, Toby. That's past two hundred. Now we walk."

Toby had no breath for speech and plodded heavily beside Amy as she counted aloud: "Eighteen. Nineteen. Twenty. Come on. Now we run."

Her energy and lightness drew him forward even as he protested, "But that's only twenty."

"That's The System. Run two hundred, walk twenty. It's called The Two Hundred–Twenty System. It will make your dreams come true. It will let you achieve your heart's desire."

"You're mad. I'm mad. This is going to kill me."

But he followed doggedly. They were just completing the third cycle of Amy's Two Hundred–Twenty System when she said, "Look … one hundred seventy-five … up ahead … one hundred-eighty … you're gaining!" Sure enough, ahead Toby saw the last of the straggling runners. "Two hundred. One, two three ... Breathe deeply, slowly, through your nose, remember ... Twelve, thirteen ... I've got to go."

"Where?"

"Back to the start — to see you finish. Nineteen, twenty. Now — *go!*"

Amy turned and sped back toward where her mother waited. Toby ran on, and as he counted for himself — fifty-four, fifty-five — he found the momentum of his counting giving momentum to his feet. And as the rhythm of his counting drove his feet — seventy-five, seventy-six — his running rhyme popped into his head again and drove them, too:

"Running feet.
Take the heat.
Won't be beat,
At the meet."

One hundred twenty-one, one hundred twenty-two, he counted to himself.

He caught up with the group of stragglers, who were now walking, and enjoyed their surprise as he chugged past. Immediately after passing them he reached two hundred, and decided, rather than walk, he'd do another two hundred and get further ahead. He was amazed at his nerve as he defied the urging of his lungs and legs to rest. He reached the next marker as he emerged from the woods, who called: "Go, big guy. That way. You're nearly there. You're doing great!"

It's like all the markers went to the same booster club, Toby muttered to himself.

Now he remembered another running rhyme, which danced in his head and in his feet:

"Here's a tale,
Of a whale

They can chase,
To no avail."

This was a joint composition by Toby and Amy. The first three lines had occurred to Toby as he jogged behind Amy on their practice run the night before. He liked the right whale and felt sorry for it, unable to outswim the old whaling boats. He imagined himself moving like a whale, surely and elegantly, if not fast. But, unlike the right whale, he'd be able to stay ahead of his pursuers.

"Here's a tale, of a whale ... They can chase ..." he'd recited to Amy, a little embarrassed, and she'd said, "Oh, Toby, it's *beauteous*."

"But I'm stuck for another line."

"We'll think of another one as we run. We'll keep repeating it while we run."

"I can't run and talk."

"I can."

"I've noticed."

"You just say it in your head, then."

It wasn't long before Amy stopped and announced: "I've got it. Wait until you hear this. Are you ready? They can chase ... *to no avail.*"

"What's *avail*?"

"No avail means they can try but they won't succeed."

"I thought *avail* was something you wore at a wedding."

"Ha ha. Funny, Toby. Come on. Let's test it. We'll say it as we run."

They'd set off, chanting as they ran,

"Here's a tale,
Of a whale
They can chase,
To no avail."

They'd found their feet flying with the rhythm of the rhyme.

Toby brought his thoughts back to the present as the rhythm of the silly rhyme…

Here's a tale,
Of a whale
They can chase,
To no avail

… drove him forward, despite the weakness he felt creeping through his body. He passed another group of runners as the last two lines repeated like the rhythm of an old-fashioned locomotive, pumping his arms like pistons:

They can chase,
To no avail.
They can chase,
To no avail…

He heard the runners behind him *(They can chase …)* as he left the woods trail to run across the park to the road, but was sure now *(To no avail…)* he could stay ahead of them.

He passed the marker who had walked him back at the last meet. The marker shouted: "You've nearly made it. That way to the finish line. Go!" As he left the park and turned on to the road for the last section of the race the last marker cupped his hands and called ahead: "Here he comes, the big guy." He could hear the feet of his pursuers pounding behind him. Now it was five minutes along the road, into the school grounds, and to the finishing line.

Panting, sides heaving, legs wobbling, telling himself through gritted teeth, "Don't stop now," Toby staggered forward, through a gathering crowd of spectators and runners which grew thicker and noisier as he approached the finishing line. The clapping and cheering grew more and more excited the closer he got to the finish. He heard cries of: "Go, go, go," and "Way to go, big guy." The faces of his mother and Conrad and Amy's mother flashed past in the crowd, his mother's astonished, Conrad's fixed with the same passion as when he watched hockey on television. He saw Mr. Walker, behind the finishing line, urging him home, heard him shouting, "Come on, Toby. Just a little more. Keep going. You're going to make it." There was Miss Little beside him, applauding with both hands high in the air as if she was at a rock concert. A thought as fleeting as the passing faces: But where's Amy? And there she was, glimpsed through the crowd, running, leaping, dancing alongside the track, keeping pace with him, her face delirious with excitement. Suddenly Derek, already long finished, burst from the crowd and ran beside him, followed by the wildly grinning and laughing twins, and Silas and Jason and Nicholas, and finally, gathering her last strength, Daphne.

Derek started to chant: "Walker's Runners. Walker's Runners," and the team joined in: "Walker's Runners. Walker's Runners."

Toby's weary legs plodded forward. He saw Mr. Walker jumping up and down, his hands high in the air one second and on his knees the next. He saw Amy alternately hugging her mother and dancing. He saw his own mother shaking her head and smiling, and beside her Conrad, grinning and pounding his fists in the air and wiggling his hips with the rhythm of the chant and Toby's failing legs: "Walker's Runners. Walker's Runners. Walker's Runners."

And at last, he crossed the finishing line.

Not last.

16

Just Toby

At recess the next day, Toby lingered in the classroom finishing some work for Ms. Watkins before he wandered outside to the playground. He was feeling curiously disconsolate, despite his success in the race, and despite Mr. Walker praising him that morning when Toby had thanked him for being coach.

Toby wondered why he felt so disconsolate. What was wrong?

He felt as if he'd lost something. That was it.

What could he have lost? What was missing?

He'd been walking slowly along one side of the playground, his head down and his hands in his pockets as he sorted through his feelings. Now he took his hands from his pockets and punched one into the other as he realised what he was missing.

He had nothing to worry about. That's what he was missing. Worry!

For the last few weeks, he realised, he'd been worrying nearly all the time about the cross-country meets. No — it wasn't so much a case of worrying, as of being keyed up, and looking forward to the practices and the meets, despite worrying about them at the same time. Now he felt … unfocussed, without direction, with nothing really on his mind.

He stood beside his old friend the dumpster. It seemed a lifetime ago that he'd spent so much time hiding behind it. He leaned against it and surveyed the playground. The older students formed patterns of constantly shifting groups as they flew from one set of friends to another. A dozen younger children were playing Red Rover on the far side of the playground, shrieking as they hurled themselves against each line. In a corner of the playground three serious games of marbles were taking place with students crouching, pointing, working out angles, contemplating tactics. In another corner the primary kids raced between the slides and the monkey bars and the ropes.

Toby wondered, *Where do I belong in all this activity?* He no longer scorned it, as he used to, but neither did he know how to join it.

He saw Daphne, standing alone beside the monkey bars, watching the little kids playing. She bent to help a kindergarten boy who fell near her, dusting him down and comforting him before he rejoined the milling children. Toby saw her gaze shift from the little children to the groups of older students, and back to the little ones. Was she really watching them, or just pretending to? Should he go and speak to her? But what would he say? Yesterday they could have talked about the cross-country meet. Today ... what?

He felt again that loss of focus and direction.

Did Daphne feel that way, too?

He edged along the dumpster. It seemed to invite him to slink behind it in order to hide his solitariness and his confusion.

The smack of a basketball on gravel, and shouted warnings, interrupted his thoughts. He hadn't noticed the basketball game going on just beyond the dumpster, where a little paved area, an oasis of smoothness amongst the gravel, boasted one basketball post and net. The ball bounced awkwardly across him. Toby instinctively put out a hand and collected it, turning smoothly as he did in the direction of the game. He looked up in time to see Jason and Nicholas, two of the players, exchange glances.

Silas, beside them, shouted, "Toby, here!"

Derek, standing under the basketball net, shouted, "Shoot, Toby."

Toby assessed the distance, said "Yeah, right," and carelessly shot the ball. It arced across the court — and landed in the net without touching the rim.

Derek said, "Wow."

The twins — he might have guessed they'd be there, too — went into a cheerleader routine, waving their arms and chanting, "Look at Toby, one and all. See him shoot the basketball."

"Toby shoots," shouted Jessica.

"Toby scores," called Jillian.

They high fived.

Silas, Nicholas and Jason were open-mouthed.

"Do it again," Silas challenged.

"No hope," said Toby.

"Try," said Derek, throwing the ball toward him.

He scooped it easily from its high bounce and, laughing, threw it toward the net. It hit the rim and bounced away.

"Look at Toby, but be nice. Knew he couldn't do it twice," the twins chanted, giggling and doing their cheerleader routine again.

Jillian grabbed the ball and dribbled it toward the net. Nicholas blocked her and she passed to Derek.

"Come on," Jason said to Toby. "It's Derek and the twins against us. We need some help. You're on our side."

"Wait. No fair," Jessica protested, standing in the middle of the court with her arms out like a policeman stopping traffic from two directions. "That makes four against three."

Toby had sudden inspiration. "Let's get Daphne. That'll make it even." He looked across the playground. Daphne was still beside the monkey bars but was looking in their direction. He wondered whether she'd been watching all the time. He waved her over to the basketball court.

* * *

When the bell screeched the end of recess Derek said to Toby, "I didn't know you were a basketball player."

"I'm not."

"You should be. Why don't you play? We start practices tomorrow. All you have to do is sign up."

The little group — Toby, with Silas and Jason on one side, Daphne on the other, the twins prancing and giggling in front, Derek and Nicholas discussing basketball tactics behind — joined the throng of students heading back into school.

* * *

Amy was playing in the road when Toby arrived home after school.

"You're just in time to play hopscotch. Come on, Toby. While you hop I want to tell you about the new project Mum and me are doing. You'll never guess what the project's on. It's on — do you want to try and guess? Do you, Toby?"

Toby said, "I guess … it's on how to talk very fast and not let your friends get a word in."

Amy said, "Ha ha. Funny, Toby. I'll tell you, anyway. It's going to be on the history of cross-country running. Did you know cross-country running started in England? Did you know that, Toby, did you? Did you know it used to be called 'hare and hounds' and it was like a paper chase? And that was in eighteen hundred and something? I bet you didn't know that, Toby. So there."

"Wow. Cool," said Toby, genuinely impressed.

"So you start hopping while I tell you what Mum and me have found out so far about the history of cross-country running."

"We've got to go up to the house first. We're going to ask Con to put up a basketball net."

"A basketball net? Why do you want Conrad to put up a basketball net, Toby?"

"So we can practise shooting baskets. I'm going to play basketball at school."

Amy put her hands on her hips.

Toby said, "Uh-oh."

Amy said sternly, "Now Toby, you've been Toby Who Hated School and Who Never Did His Work. And then you were Toby Who Was Mad At Everyone Because It Was Mr. Walker And Not Toby Who Telephoned For Help When I Had An Asthma Attack. I'm saying these in capitals, Toby. Then you turned into Toby the Cross Country Runner and Toby the Student Who Did Most Of His Work. Now are you telling me there's going to be a new Toby ... Toby the Basketball Player?"

"No," Toby protested. "I thought about all that, about being Toby the ... the ... the ... Overweight Runner, and about being Toby the Wisecracking Class Clown, and all that. Then I decided I didn't have to be Toby the Anything. I could be just Toby. I've always been just Toby. So I'm still ... just Toby."

He nodded and smiled.

Amy smiled, too.

Other books you'll enjoy in the Sports Stories series ...

Baseball

☐ *Curve Ball* by John Danakas #1
Tom Poulos is looking forward to a summer of baseball in Toronto until his mother puts him on a plane to Winnipeg.

☐ *Baseball Crazy* by Martyn Godfrey #10
Rob Carter wins an all-expenses-paid chance to be bat boy at the Blue Jays spring training camp in Florida.

☐ *Shark Attack* by Judi Peers #25
The East City Sharks have a good chance of winning the county championship until their arch rivals get a tough new pitcher.

☐ *Hit and Run* by Dawn Hunter and Karen Hunter #35
Glen Thomson is a talented pitcher, but as his ego inflates, team morale plummets. Will he learn from being benched for losing his temper?

☐ *Power Hitter* by C. A. Forsyth #41
Connor's summer was looking like a write-off. That is, until he discovered his secret talent.

☐ *Sayonara, Sharks* by Judi Peers #48
Ben and Kate are excited about the school trip to Japan, but Matt's not sure he wants to go.

Basketball

☐ *Fast Break* by Michael Coldwell #8
Moving from Toronto to small-town Nova Scotia was rough, but when Jeff makes the school basketball team he thinks things are looking up.

☐ *Camp All-Star* by Michael Coldwell #12
In this insider's view of a basketball camp, Jeff Lang encounters some unexpected challenges.

☐ *Nothing but Net* by Michael Coldwell #18
The Cape Breton Grizzly Bears prepare for an out-of-town basketball tournament they're sure to lose.

☐ *Slam Dunk* by Steven Barwin and Gabriel David Tick #23
In this sequel to *Roller Hockey Blues*, Mason Ashbury's basketball team adjusts to the arrival of some new players: girls.

☐ *Courage on the Line* by Cynthia Bates #33
After Amelie changes schools, she must confront difficult former teammates in an extramural match.

☐ *Free Throw* by Jacqueline Guest #34
Matthew Eagletail must adjust to a new school, a new team and a new father along with five pesky sisters.

☐ *Triple Threat* by Jacqueline Guest #38
Matthew's cyber-pal Free Throw comes to visit, and together they face a bully on the court.

☐ *Queen of the Court* by Michele Martin Bossley #40
What happens when the school's fashion queen winds up on the basketball court?

☐ *Shooting Star* by Cynthia Bates #46
Quyen is dealing with a troublesome teammate on her new basketball team, as well as trouble at home. Her parents seem haunted by something that happened in Vietnam.

☐ *Home Court Advantage* by Sandra Diersch #51
Debbie had given up hope of being adopted, until the Lowells came along. Adoption means moving, and making the basketball team at her new school helps. That is, until Debbie is accused of stealing from the team.

Figure Skating

☐ *A Stroke of Luck* by Kathryn Ellis #6
Strange accidents are stalking one of the skaters at the Millwood Arena.

☐ *The Winning Edge* by Michele Martin Bossley #28
Jennie wants more than anything to win a gruelling series of competitions, but is success worth losing her friends?

☐ *Leap of Faith* by Michele Martin Bossley #36
Amy wants to win at any cost, until an injury makes skating almost impossible. Will she go on?

Gymnastics

☐ *The Perfect Gymnast* by Michele Martin Bossley #9
Abby's new friend has all the confidence she needs, but she also has a serious problem that nobody but Abby seems to know about.

Ice Hockey

☐ *Two Minutes for Roughing* by Joseph Romain #2
As a new player on a tough Toronto hockey team, Les must fight to fit in.

☐ *Hockey Night in Transcona* by John Danakas #7
Cody Powell gets promoted to the Transcona Sharks' first line, bumping out the coach's son, who's not happy with the change.

☐ *Face Off* by C. A. Forsyth #13
A talented hockey player finds himself competing with his best friend for a spot on a select team.

☐ *Hat Trick* by Jacqueline Guest #20
The only girl on an all-boy hockey team works to earn the captain's respect and her mother's approval.

☐ *Hockey Heroes* by John Danakas #22
A left-winger on the thirteen-year-old Transcona Sharks adjusts to a new best friend and his mom's boyfriend.

☐ *Hockey Heat Wave* by C. A. Forsyth #27
In this sequel to *Face Off*, Zack and Mitch run into trouble when it looks as if only one of them will make the select team at hockey camp.

☐ *Shoot to Score* by Sandra Richmond #31
Playing defense on the B list alongside the coach's mean-spirited son is a tough obstacle for Steven to overcome, but he perseveres and changes his luck.

☐ *Rookie Season* by Jacqueline Guest #42
What happens when a boy wants to join an all-girl hockey team?

☐ *Brothers on Ice* by John Danakas #44
Brothers Dylan and Deke both want to play goal for the same team.

☐ *Rink Rivals* by Jacqueline Guest #49
A move to Calgary finds the Evans twins pitted against each other on the ice, and struggling to help each other out of trouble.

☐ *Power Play* by Michele Martin Bossley #50
An early-season injury causes Zach Thomas to play timidly, and a school bully is just making matters worse. Zach hopes a famous hockey player will be able to help him sort things out.

Riding

☐ *A Way with Horses* by Peter McPhee #11
A young Alberta rider, invited to study show jumping at a posh local riding school, uncovers a secret.

☐ *Riding Scared* by Marion Crook #15
A reluctant new rider struggles to overcome her fear of horses.

☐ *Katie's Midnight Ride* by C. A. Forsyth #16
An ambitious barrel racer finds herself without a horse weeks before her biggest rodeo.

☐ *Glory Ride* by Tamara L. Williams #21
Chloe Anderson fights memories of a tragic fall for a place on the Ontario Young Riders Team.

☐ *Cutting It Close* by Marion Crook #24
In this novel about barrel racing, a young rider finds her horse is in trouble just as she's about to compete in an important event.

☐ *Shadow Ride* by Tamara L. Williams #37
Bronwen has to choose between competing aggressively for herself or helping out a teammate.

Roller Hockey

☐ Roller Hockey Blues by Steven Barwin and Gabriel David Tick #17
Mason Ashbury faces a summer of boredom until he makes the roller hockey team.

Running

☐ *Fast Finish* by Bill Swan #30
Noah is a promising young runner headed for the provincial finals when he suddenly decides to withdraw from the event.

Sailing

☐ *Sink or Swim* by William Pasnak #5
Dario can barely manage the dog paddle, but thanks to his mother he's spending the summer at a water sports camp.

Soccer

☐ *Lizzie's Soccer Showdown* by John Danakas #3
When Lizzie asks why the boys and girls can't play together, she finds herself the new captain of the soccer team.

☐ *Alecia's Challenge* by Sandra Diersch #32
Thirteen-year-old Alecia has to cope with a new school, a new stepfather and friends who have suddenly discovered the opposite sex.

☐ *Shut-Out!* by Camilla Reghelini Rivers #39
David wants to play soccer more than anything, but will the new coach let him?

☐ *Offside!* by Sandra Diersch #43
Alecia has to confront a new girl who drives her teammates crazy.

☐ *Heads Up!* by Dawn Hunter and Karen Hunter #45
Do the Warriors really need a new, hot-shot player who skips practice?

☐ *Off the Wall* by Camilla Reghelini Rivers #52
Lizzie loves indoor soccer, and she's thrilled when her little sister gets into the sport. But when their teams are pitted against each other, Lizzie can only warn her sister to watch out.

Swimming

☐ *Breathing Not Required* by Michele Martin Bossley #4
Gracie works so hard to be chosen for the solo at synchronized swimming that she almost loses her best friend in the process.

☐ *Water Fight!* by Michele Martin Bossley #14
Josie's perfect sister is driving her crazy, but when she takes up swimming — Josie's sport — it's too much to take.

☐ *Taking a Dive* by Michele Martin Bossley #19
Josie holds the provincial record for the butterfly, but in this sequel to *Water Fight!* she can't seem to match her own time and might not go on to the nationals.

☐ *Great Lengths* by Sandra Diersch #26
Fourteen-year-old Jessie decides to find out whether the rumours about a new swimmer at her Vancouver club are true.

☐ *Pool Princess* by Michele Martin Bossley #47
In this sequel to *Breathing Not Required*, Gracie must deal with a bully on the new synchro team that she joins in Calgary.

Track and Field

☐ *Mikayla's Victory* by Cynthia Bates #29
Mikayla must compete against her friend if she wants to represent her school at an important track event.